.Troy

Aegean

IONIA

Samos

Sea

.Miletus

Naxos

Astypalaea

Rhodes

.Heraklion

CRETE

THE AVENGER

THE AVENGER

Margaret Hodges

Charles Scribner's Sons

NEW YORK

Library of Congress Cataloging in Publication Data
Hodges, Margaret.   The avenger.
Summary: Fifteen-year-old Alexis, son of the
ruling family of the ancient Greek city of Asini,
becomes obsessed with his quest for vengeance
against his family's enemies, until he finds him-
self fighting side-by-side with one of them at the
Battle of Marathon.
1. Greece—History—Persian Wars, 500–449 B.C.—
Juvenile fiction. [1. Greece—History—Persian
Wars, 500–449 B.C.—Fiction] I. Title.
PZ7.H664Av   1982   [Fic]   82–10246
ISBN 0–684–17636–X

Printed in the United States of America

In honor of Marathons,
for
Fletch, Art, and Johnny
whose father, too, is a good man
for the long distance race

Throughout life, the soul is engaged in an athletic contest, and when the contest is over, it meets with its reward.

PLUTARCH (c. 46–120 A.D.)

Know ye not that they which run in a race run all, but one receiveth the prize? So run, that ye may obtain . . . Now they do it to obtain a corruptible crown; but we an incorruptible.

ST. PAUL (died c. 67 A.D.)

Contents

A Note to the Reader

THE STORY of *The Avenger* takes place in ancient Greece, beginning with the Olympic Games of 492 B.C. and ending with the battle of Marathon, fought against the armies of the Persian king Darius the Great, in September, 490 B.C. After the Persian Wars came the Golden Age of Greek civilization that gave us a priceless heritage of philosophy, architecture, sculpture, drama, science, literature, and a view of life that Rome was to pass on to western Europe, and finally to the English-speaking world.

This flowering of Hellenic culture owed a great debt to the valiant stand by ten thousand Athenians and a thousand Plataeans who had pushed the invading Persian army into the sea at Marathon; it was one of the decisive battles of the world. A Persian victory would have meant the domination of Asiatic over Hellenic culture, and rule by tyranny instead of rule by law agreed upon by free men. An important aspect of Marathon was that slaves for the first time won their liberty by fighting shoulder to shoulder with free citizens. Alexis, my fictional hero, was one of these slaves.

Herodotus, who has been called the father of history, wrote about the thrilling events of the Persian Wars; and the Greek traveler Pausanias later gave detailed descriptions of the famous sites to which Alexis's road led him. Today, tourist buses take the traveler to these ancient landmarks. At Olympia we see where the Games began. As we wander through the ruins of Epidauros, shrine of the merciful god Asklepios who healed the sick, we remember that doctors still use the sign of Asklepios's staff with serpents twined around it. The walls of Tiryns even now look as if giants had built them. In the museums of Athens, breathtaking treasures of ancient Greece are gathered. The marketplace (the Agora) is being restored, and the High City (the Acropolis) crowns the modern city, defying the ravages of time, wars, and neglect. Twenty-six miles to the northeast of Athens, the funeral mounds for the heroes remain where

The mountains look on Marathon
And Marathon looks on the sea . . .

Asini, on the Peloponnese, the southern part of the mainland of Greece, was barely mentioned by ancient historians and travelers. But Homer listed Asini among the cities that sent ships to Troy, and he praised the youthful daring of the leader, Diomedes. The ruins of Asini can be found about five miles southeast from Nauplion, above a bay so beautiful that if you see it once, you will long to return. Recent excavations by Swedish archeologists have shown that the town was occupied during the time when I have pictured it as the home of Alexis.

All the characters in this story are fictional except for a few important Athenians: Aeschylus, the first of the great Greek tragic dramatists; Miltiades, commander-in-chief at Marathon; Pheidippides, the runner of the first "Marathon race"; and Themistocles, the military strategist who built the Athenian navy in time for its conclusive victory against the Persian navy of Xerxes at Salamis in 480 B.C. Aesop might have been living in these years.

The immortal Homer had been dead for several centuries, but he seemed very much alive. His words were the text for every schoolboy's lessons and were quoted as the Bible would be quoted in the Judeo-Christian era. In his spirited book *The Greeks*,* Professor H. D. F. Kitto points out that because these amazing people "were soaked in Homer from their youth up, [they knew] that the quality of a man matters more than his achievement; that violence and recklessness will still lead to disaster, and that this will fall on the innocent as well as on the guilty," so long as human life lasts. All of this wisdom Alexis, the avenger, learned along the road laid out for him by the gods, from Asini to Marathon.

---

* Kitto, H.D.F. *The Greeks*. Harmondsworth, Middlesex: Penguin [1951].

·I·

From Asini

· 1 ·

ALL NIGHT the great west wind, the rainy wind of spring, blew down from the mountains, and the sea god's horses thundered on the beach. Alexis, half awake, heard the gusts of rain flung relentlessly against the flat roof of his father's house, until toward morning the wind changed and the weather began to clear. In the silence that followed the storm, Alexis slept deeply. When he woke, refreshed, the small east window framed the morning star in a sky washed with light, and the peaks of the islands in the bay stood black against the glow.

Seeing his brother's bed empty in the far corner of the room, Alexis judged that Dion had gone to find Telamon, their tutor and trainer, who preferred to box with his young Olympic contestant early in the day, before other duties took their toll of his energy. Boxing had been Telamon's own sport in the days when he had been a free man. He said that he knew nothing about running but that it was simple enough. Alexis could teach himself by starting every day with a run on the beach.

It was time for that run. Throwing off his blanket, Alexis pulled his tunic over his head and left the room. His bare feet made no sound on the stone floor as he circled the balcony. The women's rooms were quiet. Behind the closed

3

doors his sister Niki must still be sleeping. But the slave quarters were empty and so was the chamber of his father and his stepmother. Aristes was the sort of master who always left his bed at first light, going the rounds of orchards, fields, and vineyards, or taking command on the beach if a ship was to be launched. His wife Melissa was sure to be up and about somewhere, like a bee, busy with her endless tasks. Melissa, a bee, thought Alexis. It was the meaning of her name, and she did make life sweet for all the family.

Alexis would find his father later, but for now, he ran down the broad steps that led to the lower level of the ancient palace. The inner courtyards were deserted as he passed through them. Only in the quarters of his grandfather Abas was there activity. He heard the old man's voice and the sound of servants preparing his early breakfast. At the porter's lodge the sleepy watchman nodded a bleary-eyed greeting and swung open the outer door.

Alexis saw before him the narrow promontory that jutted southward into the bay. In time long past, before the Greeks had sailed against Troy, the men of Asini had topped this peak with a stone tower that still guarded the palace from attack by sea. Alexis stood for a moment and, looking about in the brightness of the spring morning, saw that all was well. The town walls of Asini protected the palace from the landward side, ending in the waters of the bay on either side of the promontory. Outside the walls, to east and west, the curved beach lay peaceful, lapped by a white froth of little waves, as if the sea god Poseidon had forgotten last night's anger and returned with his swift horses to his own palace, glistening and golden, in the depths of the wine-dark sea. On the horizon all around rose the mountains, range behind range, gray in the morning light. It was a perfect morning for a run.

There were two ways to the beach, through stone tunnels that led down, inside the town walls, each ending with a guarded door at the water's level. A pair of his father's ships were careened on the westward beach, and sailors were at work there, so Alexis chose the tunnel to the eastward gate and ordered the guard to open it. He emerged onto the firm, smooth sand, dropped his tunic, and, setting his feet in the stone grooves that marked the starting line, began his run just as the rim of the mountains caught fire in the sunrise. He was hardly conscious of his body, as if the harmony of sky, mountains, and sea were part of him and he a part of the whole.

He should ask nothing more of the gods, he thought, than to be alive on this day, and to run. Yet as he ran, without a conscious thought except for his pace and style, his will, like an unspoken prayer, was set on something more, and had been set from earliest childhood. What he wanted was revenge against his father's enemy, Neleus of Tiryns, and revenge against Glaukon, Neleus's only son. If possible, Alexis wanted to destroy the entire city of Tiryns. He had often seen its mighty walls in the distance while hunting in the hills with his father. If he could not bring down those walls, he could at least vow to destroy the heir to the throne of Tiryns. How this could be done he did not yet know, but it was a sacred duty to try. Tiryns and Asini had always been rival cities, and five years ago a terrible event had increased their enmity as never before. Aristes, returning home from a trading voyage, had been attacked by pirates. Putting out from many ports on the coast of Asia, they were a constant threat. The fight had taken place within sight of another Greek ship, commanded by Neleus of Tiryns, and Neleus had sailed on, making no effort to help. Aristes's ship had sunk, his sailors drowned, and he had lost a fortune in cargo. He alone had managed by a miracle to swim to shore, but he had been living in debt ever since. If his creditors became impatient, they could have him sold into slavery for his debts. To avenge Neleus's act of cowardice or deliberate malice, no matter which, was laid on the shoulders of Dion and Alexis as well as Aristes. Unavenged, the disaster hung like a curse over all Asini—men, women, and children—and especially over the family of Aristes. The coming revenge was always at the back of Alexis's mind, even in his happiest moments.

Now, as he ran, he prayed that he might win the boys' race at Olympia at the end of the summer, but even more he prayed that his brother Dion might win a victory in the boxing against Glaukon, son of Neleus. In another four years Alexis would be a man. Then, if Glaukon still lived, Alexis would enter some other event against him. Sometimes he pictured himself defeating Glaukon in all five events of the pentathlon: running, the discus and the javelin throw, the long jump, and wrestling. Even better, Alexis might start training for the pankration, the boxing and wrestling in which brutal, damaging injuries were allowed. He saw Glaukon lying crushed under his foot after the pankration. In time, Alexis and Dion together at their father's side would wipe out the score against Neleus. They would begin with victories over Glaukon at Olympia, and in the end they would avenge completely the wrong done by Neleus, or die in the attempt.

Alexis's run, a stade's length as at Olympia, brought him to the stone finish line set in sand. There he walked about, flexing his muscles, well satisfied. The morning star

6

had faded and the sun had risen. The encircling mountains and the islands, smoothly breasting the waters of the bay, raised their dark, familiar shapes into high blue space. At the top of the nearest island stood a shrine to Poseidon. It was small, and old enough to have watched the black ships when they had lined the shore seven hundred years ago, ready to be launched for Troy. Aristes had often talked of building a fine new temple to the sea god, but it had never been possible. Since the disaster, all that he could scratch together went to pay his debts to the foreign merchants whose goods had gone down in the shipwreck. Thinking of his father's debts, Alexis raised his arms toward the island and vowed to build the new shrine if Poseidon would help him take revenge on Neleus and his son Glaukon. He saw his own shadow stretched giant-sized on the golden sand. So a god might look, vowing revenge, thought Alexis; but he was no god, only a human, and he would need super-human help. He did not see himself even as a hero; the younger son, the younger brother—that was his role.

The boy who cast the long shadow was not as tall as he wanted to be. His youthful arms and thighs were still smoothly muscled, his shoulders not yet as broad as a man's. But his face was strong, and handsomer than he knew. His brows arched above a fine straight nose; his mouth was firm. His dark hair curled on his well-shaped head. He was in training to honor his gods, his town, and his family, and he intended to do his best.

He had turned back to begin the return sprint, which he would do at full speed, when he saw a girl racing toward him, tunic tied short, and long fair hair flying behind her. It was Niki. She was already thirteen, too old to be here on the beach, alone and running like that. No other girl in Asini behaved so. But she ran well, so easily, so

7

lightly, and so fast. Watching her through narrowed eyes, he had to admit it. Atalanta, in the old story, must have looked the same when she raced with her suitors and outran all of them, except the last.

Niki came up to him, panting and laughing. "How was that? Did I do well?"

His answer was curt. "Does our mother know where you are?"

Niki looked up at him with a teasing smile. "Of course not." In this mood her voice was always as sweet as a run of notes on a lyre.

"She should give you a beating."

"She never will."

"And as a result, you give nothing but trouble. They should have called you Pandora. I pity the man who marries you—if our father can find you a husband. Useless, and a trouble-maker, that's what you are. How will you manage a house if you are married?"

"The servants will do the work."

"What if you have no servants?"

"My father would not marry me to a man who had no servants."

"And who would show the servants what to do?"

"My husband's mother."

"But what will *you* do?"

"Be beautiful, so that my husband will love me."

"Even Helen of Troy ended with no one to love her."

"I won't mind. Besides, do you think I am ready to be shut up forever in a house?"

"I know you are not," he said sternly. "You are ready for nothing. You have the body of a woman and the mind of a child, disobedient and full of curiosity, fit for nothing but play. You even keep your old toys."

She turned away, pouting. "It's not true. I have given my toys to Artemis. You see, you don't know all about me. One day—it was months ago—I carried them all to the spring and said a prayer to the goddess and dropped them in. All but my doll."

Alexis laughed.

She sat down, kicking at the sand with her heels. Disobedient, curious, and good for nothing. That described his sister, except for one more quality: her perfect beauty. She had that too, or so it seemed to Alexis, comparing her with the glimpses he had had of other girls at festivals and ceremonies, where they remained shy and silent within protective family groups.

A stroke of fate had made Niki what she was. Aristes had named her for the beautiful mother who had died giving birth to her, and he denied her nothing. He had not married again for ten years. His business as a trader took him away from home for months at a time, and during these long absences he had left his home and family in the care of his own father and mother. The arrangement satisfied him, or so he said, but his children knew that their mother had been the real love of his life and was irreplaceable.

It had taken ten years for Aristes to realize what everyone else had long seen, that the grandparents were too old to go on carrying the responsibility for his household as well as for two sons and a daughter. Dion had finished his two years of military training, but now he lived only for boxing. He had learned nothing about the farm, or the sea trading, and was therefore of no use. Alexis admired his older brother without reservation but found in him no model to follow. Then there was Niki, willful, hopelessly willful, and ignorant. Every year she grew more beautiful, with skin the color of a peach ripened in the sun, and eyes the northern blue not often seen in the Peloponnese. "Like her mother," said Gorgo, who had nursed all the children. "Niki has perfect teeth and beautiful legs. The picture of her mother." But the adoring old nurse could not control Niki.

Before Melissa had come, bringing order and seemliness to the household, Niki had never spun a skein of wool or woven a length of cloth, knew nothing of the kitchen, and could not read or write her own name. Melissa was trying by gentle means to teach her and to prepare her for a woman's life, but the going was hard for both of them. Niki still did much as she pleased and spent time every day training herself for the girls' races, run at Olympia in years between the great Games. Considering her speed and skill, the goal was not impossible, and she had at least won a point. Her father had promised that she should go to Olympia at the end of the summer. Naturally, she would not watch the Games—there was a death penalty for any woman who did that—but, well guarded by Gorgo, she could have the pleasure of the voyage and see the arrival of the athletes in procession. Melissa had not asked or wished to go to Olympia. At long last she was with child and expected her confinement before the winter.

Suddenly Niki was on her feet and running back along the beach as she called over her shoulder, "Race with me."

Alexis soon outdistanced her. At the foot of the promontory he turned and watched her coming, flushed and joyous with the exercise, only a moment behind him. After all, how lovely, and loveable, she was. And if she wanted to run, where could she do it but on the beach? They were friends again as they climbed the tunnel path to the palace and went their separate ways.

Alexis found his grandparents at a table in their sunny courtyard, making a small meal of porridge and sweet figs. The rest of the family began their day without breaking their fast, but the old people wanted their morning food. Abas often said, "At the end, there is not much else we can enjoy." He said it now, shaking with silent laughter, his deep eyes glinting under shaggy brows, and added that he had presents for Dion and Alexis. They must come to see him later in the day. Alexis promised, and sat down to eat a handful of figs. His grandmother, Chrysis, kept her usual monumental silence, but he felt her brooding pride in him, and her affection.

There were three Fates in his family, Alexis thought. Chrysis, with her face almost always hidden under the shelter of her dark veil, was the old one who cut the thread at the end of life. When anyone died in the house, or on the farm, free man or slave, it was Chrysis who directed the preparation of the body for burial. She took constant care of Abas, as if she knew that his days were numbered. She trimmed his white hair and beard, and got down on her old knees to tie his sandals. As he grew more and more frail, no one else could make him so comfortable. Abas had been known to kick over the basin of water that Gorgo brought each evening for the washing of his feet. The woman was a fool, he said, and the water always too hot or too cold, unless Chrysis had tested it.

Yet, as Abas became fretful in his weakness, no one in the family failed in respect and affection. They remembered him as he had been, the magic teller of tales, with voice and lyre bringing back Diomedes of the loud war cry, and all the Greek heroes of the Peloponnese who had followed Diomedes to Troy from Argos, and Tiryns, and Asini. It was Abas who had taught his son and grandsons

11

the first lines of Homer they ever knew by heart: "When you have got to the place of battle, where the best men fight, do not bring shame on your father's house, or on us who in time past have been famous for strength and courage over all the world."

It was sad to see Abas now. He was another child for Gorgo to nurse. In the family of Aristes, as long as Alexis could remember, Gorgo had been the Fate whose fingers spun and shaped the tender thread of life.

To Alexis, his stepmother Melissa, whom he called mother, was the third Fate. It was she who wove the lives of all the household into a fabric both warm and beautiful. Having kissed the hands of his grandparents, he went to find Melissa in the women's quarters, where the day's work was now well under way. One of the young slave girls sat on the bench before a small loom that was half-filled with a length of apple-green wool. She had somehow snarled her thread and was looking up in appeal, but without fear, as the mistress untangled the shuttle and set it free. Alexis saw why Melissa managed things so well whenever her husband was away, and why her orders were so willingly obeyed. He said to her, smiling, "I think you could untangle every trouble in the world."

"If only I could," she said with an answering smile, and seemed to relax in the warmth of his approval.

Alexis knew most, if not all, of what there was to know about Melissa. She came from Crete, an only daughter of good family. Her father had not sought a marriage for her because he depended on her for the management of his domestic affairs, the wife being an invalid. The father was a trader and had invited Aristes to his house in Heraklion, where Aristes had met the quiet, gentle daughter. Well taught and living in a city famous for its culture, she was more than suitable as a stepmother for his children. She was no longer in her first youth, but her large dark eyes and sweetly curving lips attracted him enough to see in her an answer to the needs of his neglected home. Since he was known as a man of substance in the port, he had persuaded the father to let Melissa go.

What she felt in her heart about her marriage was unknown to anyone but herself. The only sign she gave was of compliant obedience to her father, and now to her husband. Aristes treated her with the respect due a wife, but at times Alexis saw her face shadowed as if by sadness. He supposed that she was homesick for Crete. As for the baby she wanted so much, perhaps this made her anxious. He knew that Melissa often bought little statues of beautiful children and kept them in the chamber she shared with his father. Now that her prayers were about to be answered, he hoped that her sadness would pass, but he did not speak to her about the expected baby. That was woman's business. Privately, he thought, "We three are enough, Dion, Niki, and I. She takes care of us. We do not need more children."

·2·

Leaving Melissa, he bathed quickly and went straight to the benches on a sunny side of the inner courtyard where Telamon met his pupils. It was a pleasant place with a fountain of fresh water that came down from the stony hills behind Asini. This year all of Telamon's pupils, except for Alexis, were boys of the town who paid for their lessons. In the morning, Telamon taught reading, writing, arithmetic, and music. In the afternoons he took his class to the gymnasium in the center of town, where he trained them in sports, according to their talents. This year there were six boys.

With the fees paid by the outsiders, Telamon would soon be able to buy his freedom from Aristes and would probably do so when Alexis became sixteen and ended his schooling. In the meantime, Telamon seemed content to teach, his face a mask of disapproval when his pupils did not please him, his cheeks wreathed in smiles when they did well. He had a passion for the idea of excellence, without ever having tried to attain it himself. He came from Samos, richest of islands, where Persian gold made Samian luxury a byword. His father was a silversmith, who had trained him in the fine points of that art and sent him to a good school, where he learned all the subjects necessary for a boy who was expected to have a bright future. Telamon had done well at school, but he had developed a wanderlust and left Samos, against his father's will, handling an oar aboard any galley that was sailing for some new port.

He said that he had set foot on every island in the Aegean and in most of the Ionian cities where Greeks had settled on the mainland of Asia. Perhaps it was true. At last he had reached Athens. He considered Athens to be the finest city in the world because of its government in which all citizens played their part. Unfortunately, Athenian citizenship was limited to men on official lists. Telamon had therefore bribed an official to put his name on a list. The deception had quickly been discovered, and Telamon had been sold into slavery as punishment. Aristes, who happened to be in the port of Athens with a cargo of goods, had seen Telamon on the auction block, and, hearing what he could do, bought him as a likely teacher and trainer for his sons.

This morning Telamon set an arithmetic lesson for a pair of twins, aged seven, who had just begun school. They were to cut an apple into sections, count the parts, and fit them together again, after which they were allowed to eat the apple. He also gave out a new passage from Homer for the older boys to learn by heart. It described the great shield of Achilles, made on the anvil of the gods. Wonderful images were hammered out on the shining metal: the earth and the sky, sea, sun, moon and stars, and all the doings of men, their work, their play, their peace and wars, their cities, farms, vineyards and flocks. The shield of Achilles showed all things and around the rim flowed the River of Ocean, the limit of the world.

When Telamon called on the older boys to recite, he was severe. Today he did not expect them to remember all of the lines, but he had his strap ready for any boy who made mistakes in reading or enunciation.

"Do not dare to mispronounce one of these words of the divine Homer. Remember that the gods themselves told him what to write." Later, he questioned them on lines from Homer about their own great hero, Diomedes of Argos, youngest of the Greek leaders at Troy, whose city dominated all others on the Argolic Gulf.

"Portes, tell us why the goddess Athene put valor into Diomedes's heart."

"She did it 'that he might excel all the others, and cover himself with glory.' "

"And how did he look?"

" 'She made a stream of fire flash from his shield and helmet like the star that shines brightest in summer after

15

rising from the sea. She kindled such a fire on his head and shoulders and sent him into the thickest of the fight.' "

"Well done, Portes. So Diomedes felt the rage of battle and the strength of a god came to his aid. You, Pyrrias, what did Diomedes say when King Agamemnon was about to give up the fight?"

"He said—he said that the Greeks should return to the fight and—and even though they were wounded—"

"But the words, Pyrrias? Give us the lines exactly."

"I can't remember them exactly."

Telamon laid on the strap with a will. "Now, Alexis, what became of Odysseus after the shipwreck?"

Alexis knew the lines perfectly and recited them without a fault. They described all too well what had happened to his own father. " 'For two nights and two days he was tossed about in the swelling sea, expecting death. But when Dawn with her fair hair brought the third day, the wind fell, and as he was lifted on a great wave, he saw land near by and swam on. When he was within earshot of the shore, and heard the thunder of the sea against the reefs, for there were no harbors or sheltered beaches, but only jutting headlands and cliffs—' "

"Enough. You have it by heart and say it with great expression and good accent." Telamon's clean-shaven cheeks creased in his subtle smile. He was well aware that every boy in the class knew what the passage meant to Alexis.

Once, in the spring of the year when Alexis was ten years old, he and Dion had been hunting with their father in the hills between Asini and Tiryns, which were about eight miles apart. They had come upon Neleus and Glaukon looking at a trap that Aristes had set the night before. Neleus's face had a look of cold pride and power, and

Alexis had instantly detested him. The two men had exchanged shouts and insults while the boys stood by, staring at each other in uneasy silence. Alexis would not soon forget how Glaukon looked, a true son of Heracles, fair-haired and as tall and broad in the shoulders as Dion. His chest was bared so that Alexis saw how the muscle and sinew moved under the smooth skin. The column of his neck was already as firm and strong as a man's and he had the big hands and feet of a youth who would grow still more. That summer, Aristes had made the fatal voyage when Neleus abandoned him to the mercies of the pirates.

Now, five years later, Dion, sombrely intent on a quick revenge at last, saw his opportunity only four months away at Olympia. Glaukon was rumored to be a fair match for him, and he, Dion, would completely humiliate him by beating him within an inch of his life. "I would kill him, except that they would disqualify me," he said.

Alexis's mind brooded over a wider problem. He, more than Dion, loved his family, the ancient palace, and every handful of earth within the walls of Asini. He had a great capacity to love. And to love was good, but to hate was also good. When he thought of Glaukon, of Glaukon's father, and the city of Tiryns, his hatred embraced them, anger rose in him like smoke, and the taste of it in his soul was sweeter than honey.

Within the memory of living man, Tiryns had always been bigger, stronger, and richer than Asini. Its walls had been built not by men but by giants, and it had a great history. The city had once been ruled by Perseus, destroyer of the monstrous Gorgon, and later by mighty Heracles, both of them sons of Zeus. It would take the help of the gods to bring Tiryns down in ruins, but the gods would find ways. Clothed in mist and invisible to mortal

17

sight, they saw the evil done by men and would not forget or be appeased until justice was done. Zeus had two jars of gifts, one filled with evil, one with good, and to most men he gave an even mixture of both. But for those who allowed a wrong to go unavenged, evil gifts were doubled. Such men lived as if polluted, and all their efforts went for nothing. So it was with Asini, and so it would be as long as Neleus and his family lived and prospered.

For the last hour of the school morning the little boys were sent home and Telamon turned to the music lesson. He devoted much time to the tuning of the lyre, because he could not bear false notes and because the tuning called attention to an idea which excited him. It seemed to Telamon no less than miraculous that there was a relationship between music and mathematics. It could be seen in the relationship between the lengths of gut strung on the lyre to produce the notes of the scale. He constantly reminded the boys that Apollo, god of the lyre, was also the god of reason, of order, and of intellect. So, if they truly understood the lyre and the laws of musical harmony, they might learn to live in harmony with the universe which, by the will of the god, gave forth the very same harmonies as the lyre. This was why the lyre was played while athletes exercised in the gymnasium. The whole body as well as the mind must move in harmony.

Telamon disapproved of the flute because it spoiled one's looks to pucker the lips and blow. He also gave perfunctory warnings to his pupils about the danger of spoiling their looks while boxing, but it was clear that he was proud to be training a boxer for the Games. Dion was not concerned that his handsome nose might be broken and flattened. "Telamon forgets that he is a slave," he said. "He should teach me to box and otherwise keep quiet." But

18

Alexis was concerned. He cared about his brother's looks.

At noon Telamon always dismissed the boys with some advice for the good of their souls. Today he gave them some lines from Hesiod, who was second only to Homer in wisdom: "Badness you can get easily; the road to it is smooth and close at hand. But between you and excellence the gods have put sweat, and the road is long and steep. It is rough at first, but even though it is hard, when you come to the top it is easy." Pyrrias, still sore from Telamon's strap, felt that this was meant for him and went home looking glum.

At noon, Alexis saw his family together for the first real meal of the day. The table was spread under the fig tree that cast a welcome shade in the intense light of midday. Aristes, home from the fields and vineyards, sat at the head of the table, cutting a great loaf of bread and mixing the wine with water. He praised the platter of fish, part of a catch brought in that morning by one of his own boats. Lettuce from the farm, freshly picked and dressed with olive oil and salt, completed the feast.

Dion, at twenty, was free to speak at the table if he wished. He reported the success of his morning, first boxing with Telamon, and later, shadow-boxing with his friends at the gymnasium. Having bathed and changed to a fresh tunic, he was looking and feeling like a young god. In the eyes of Alexis, Dion *was* godlike: the firstborn, and a better man than he would ever be. Dion was very like their father. Alexis, looking from one to the other, saw the same powerful shoulders and erect bearing, the same air of calm command. When they practiced throwing the javelin in the afternoons at the stadium, either of them could have posed for a statue of Poseidon hurling his spear.

But there was a difference between Aristes and Dion.

Where the son wanted only to excel in boxing, the father took pleasure in doing everything well. In Asini he was judge, and he was king. He had a passion for his ships and the sea. He often went out with his fishing boats, as delighted to bring in a good catch as if he were still a boy. The herdsmen respected his advice because he knew sheep and cattle as well as they did. He went into the hills with friends, a skillful hunter of the wild animals that plagued his flocks. After a morning's work on the farm, he would ride across country for practice, choosing the roughest and steepest ground, leaping ditches and canals, following as closely as he could the conditions of war, to be ready if it came. He tried, without success, to teach Dion all that he knew, but Dion's heart was in the palestra, not in trading or farming. It was Alexis who always begged to go to the farm and who followed at his father's heels as he went about the barns, the orchard, and the vineyard, or lent a hand with the ploughing.

Now Aristes sat at ease, giving Abas a report on the farm. The cattle were thriving and there were two new calves. Tomorrow he would be sending a shipload of spring lambs to Nauplion. Yes, the plowing had begun and he had not forgotten to offer the proper sacrifices for a good harvest. The orchards and vineyards promised well. When winter came, there would be plenty, and with a few good cargoes he might be able to pay some of his creditors. On this happy note the family went to their afternoon rest.

Late in the day Aristes went to the gymnasium with Dion and Alexis. He stripped for a brief bout of wrestling, not too strenuous, with a friend, Demeus, and then retired to the hot bath. When he emerged, his skin smooth and glowing from a good rubdown, he went to join other friends who stood watching the exercises of the younger men. Alexis, who had won a sprint against some boys of his age, saw his father with Demeus, approaching a circle where Telamon was telling tales that he had heard on his travels.

"This is not your work," Aristes said to him brusquely. "Go to Dion."

When Telamon had taken himself off to the boxing arena, Aristes added with a shrug, "That man is all talk, most of it clever, I grant you, but too clever for his own good. He pretends to have all the gossip from foreign courts and says he repeats the stories only to amuse us, as Aesop did. I tell him that he will end like Aesop by offending someone important and being thrown over a cliff."

Demeus laughed. "You must admit that the stories are memorable. You've heard the one about Cambyses's chair?"

"A dozen times."

Alexis, too, had heard that story. According to Telamon, Cambyses, who had followed Cyrus the Great as king of Persia, liked little jokes. He had put a Greek judge in control of affairs along the seacoast where Ionian Greeks lived. Later, he accused the judge of taking bribes and had him killed. The man's skin was flayed, cut into strips, and made into a judgment-seat. Cambyses then made the man's son judge in his father's place but told him that when he sat in his judgment-seat, he should not forget what he was sitting on.

"I think that Telamon exaggerates the threat from Asia," said Demeus. "All of that was years ago, and far away, if it ever happened. In any case, Ionia does not concern me. We have enough to do defending Asini from Tiryns." Aristes agreed.

It was almost nightfall when Dion and Alexis went to their grandfather. He was sitting by the fire in his own room, where he kept the treasures of a lifetime. He had his lyre and a roll of parchment beside his chair, and he came to the point at once.

"You know my days are almost past. No, don't deny it. You can still guess what I once was, as the stubble field shows what the grain has been, but my strength is going. My fingers are too stiff to handle the lyre and my eyes too dim to read poems. Dion, I give the lyre to you. You are a boxer and have not shown much taste for music. But boxing is not enough. You should learn the old songs. There is truth in them, and they link the living and the dead. It is right that you, the firstborn, should give your children the truth that has been given to you, but you cannot give what you don't have. Alexis, I give you the words of the best songs that I know. You may not need to have them written down because I think you will learn them by heart . . . you have a talent for poetry. But it has come to me in a dream that you will travel far and cannot take a lyre where you are going. Those who come afterward may need to have the words written down. My sword and spear I leave for the one who needs them."

When his grandsons had thanked him and kissed his cheek, he dismissed them with a wave of his hand.

Two weeks later, on a day so warm that bees were buzzing around Melissa's flowers in the great courtyard, Abas went down to the beach for a walk. He took no servant, being in a mood to say that the slaves were more hindrance than help. When he did not return in time for the evening meal, Alexis was sent to look for him. On the eastern beach he found his grandfather lying face down in the shallow water. The tide was coming in.

All that night and the next day the women of the palace wailed in the ceremony of mourning, and the family ritually sheared their hair. But the mourning was more than ceremony and ritual. The death of Abas brought a break in the family circle and all felt it deeply. Old Chrysis could only say, "I had to let him go. He wanted to go." It was Aristes who searched through his memory and found the right words to comfort them. "Remember how Odysseus looked forward to his death? 'From the sea will come my death, the gentlest death. It will end me, worn smooth with old age, and my people shall live happily around the place where I lie.' So it is with Abas. Think of him in the Happy Isles—the quiet garden, the apple tree, the singing, and the gold. He is young again. He races his chariot, and he sings praise to the gods with an immortal lyre."

They dug a grave for Abas on the promontory high above the bay and a priest of Poseidon came from the little island to chant prayers. The fragrant smoke of incense rose in the clear air as Aristes poured the libation and offered the sacrificial lamb. One of his freemen, an artist, was set to work carving a monument in stone to stand by the grave.

At the time of the next full moon Alexis and Dion were to sail with Telamon for Elis, north of Olympia, where they would have a final month of intensive training before the Games. They were looking forward to this when, soon after the death of Abas, on a morning of stainless sky and sparkling sea, a tall, fair-haired young man knocked at the landward gate of Asini. He announced himself as Glaukon, son of Neleus of Tiryns, and demanded to see Aristes. He was taken under guard to the inner courtyard of the palace to wait for the arrival of the master, who was not yet home from the fields.

As Glaukon stood with folded arms, looking about, Niki came into the courtyard to fill a water jar at the fountain. Alexis, hearing of Glaukon's arrival, went to meet him. He saw his sister, her shorn head covered with a veil, bending to fill the jar. She lifted it to her shoulder, turned, and paused, startled by the presence of the stranger. Alexis saw that her eyes met Glaukon's. Then she was gone.

Alexis stared coldly at Glaukon. "I know who you are," he said. "What do you want?"

Glaukon returned the stare. "To be brief, my father's huntsmen found a man of Asini taking a deer from one of our nets. There was a fight, and the man is dead. I have brought his body back to your town. I am to tell your father to warn all Asinian thieves."

"Listen to me," Alexis broke in. "Give orders to others, not to us. I will tell my father what you have said, and I will tell you something. Keep it in mind. If you come here again, I will kill you."

·II·

To Olympia

·1·

ARLY in the summer, three heralds from Elis arrived
at Asini. They were one delegation among many
who were making their rounds of all the Greek
states. They came in splendid chariots, preceded by trumpets and banners and followed by a company of public
trainers and judges. They announced the beginning of the
sacred truce that stopped hostilities between Greek city-
states who were sending contestants to the Olympic Games.
All Greek citizens were invited to attend.

This year Asini had no contestants for the pentathlon,
for wrestling, or for the pankration. Nor would the town
compete in the events that involved great expense, the
chariot race and the horse race. Aristes could not afford
such an outlay, and his financial problems had a depress-
ing effect on the fortunes of the entire town. Prayers of
thanksgiving were offered that at least Dion was judged fit
to compete in the boxing, and Alexis in the boys' race.

On the morning before the full moon of midsummer
all of Asini, men, women, and children, came down to the
beach to watch the ship sail for Elis. As Aristes and his
family came in procession from the palace, the ship rode at
anchor near shore, loaded with food and supplies, and men

of the town were already manning the oars. It was time for the final farewells.

Melissa gave each of the boys a small parcel wrapped in soft cloths. "Find the right altars for these," she said, "wherever you think best." Her anxious eyes added, "Take care of yourselves." She did not speak the words, but the voice of Aristes rang out so that all could hear: "May a fair wind carry you on your way and may all the gods watch over you."

Townsmen lifted his sons shoulder-high and carried them out to the ship, while Telamon, carrying his own bundles, waded behind and clambered on board after them. The crowd laughed and cheered. Then Niki, forgetting all modesty, ran to the water's edge. As the oars began to move in rhythm, her voice, high and sweet, called from the shore, "I will see you at Olympia." For once, no one seemed to be reprimanding her.

The shipmaster soon raised the sail. When he learned that this was the first long voyage for the king's sons, he explained the course to them, tracing the route in the air with a forefinger. "Once we have crossed our gulf, we will be hugging the shore southward to the land's end. There we head west to the Ionian sea, then north to Elis. Sometimes we will be out of sight of land . . . at least a week's voyage."

Telamon, stretched at ease in the shadow of the sail, sighed with satisfaction.

"And you, my fine friend," said the shipmaster, "will take your turn at the oars."

Telamon showed no enthusiasm. "When I was a free man, I rowed with the best," he said. "But the divine Homer speaks the truth—'Zeus takes away half a man's strength the day he becomes a slave.' I am here as trainer and teacher of the king's sons and must save my strength for that."

Propped against the mast, he talked to anyone who would listen. He harked back to other voyages he had made along the coast of Asia. "You foolish Asinians! You say that Asia is far away, but Asian memories are long. They have not forgotten the fall of Troy, and they want revenge against all Greece. You think only of your own affairs and your own little wars. Wait until King Darius comes upon us, as he will do. He has already taken Samos. And you have heard of Miletus, you young ones? No? It is on the mainland of Asia, near my island of Samos. Miletus has been Greek for five hundred years, and within your lifetime it led a revolt of all the Ionian Greek cities, to free them from Persian rule. Surely your father has told you? You should know that Athens came to the aid of Miletus and even burned Darius's city of Sardis, with the help of only one ally, little Eretria."

"Where is Eretria?" asked Alexis.

"It is on the island of Euboea, across the straits from Marathon, which is twenty-six miles north of Athens. You have at least heard of Marathon, if only because the divine Theseus fought a great bull there." Alexis knew that story.

"Well," Telamon went on, "Darius had to fight for six years before he brought the Ionian Greeks to their knees. Now the story goes that he shot an arrow straight up into the air and prayed, 'Almighty god, give me revenge against the Athenians!' He has ordered a servant to say to him every day, 'Remember the Athenians!' Oh, he will come, believe me, he will come. One day he will be hammering at the walls of Athens, and the next he will be at Asini." Telamon's constant stream of talk helped to pass the time, but no one was much impressed.

All day the ship moved southward along a rugged and thinly settled coast where mountains stretched out from the mainland far into the sea. At nightfall, seeing no sign of human life, they dropped anchor close to a small beach and made a meal of fish, olives, and barley cake. They slept on the sand, wrapped in their cloaks.

The next night they were luckier. Before dark, a thread of smoke appeared on a slope close to shore, and when they dropped anchor, they heard a dog barking. A goat path led up to a small house in a clearing where a man and his wife welcomed the travelers and made them comfortable for the night. There was fresh water from a mountain stream and vegetables from a little garden. The woman stirred up the fire under a pot of soup that would have lasted her husband and herself for a week. "Strangers are from the gods," their host said, "and I can see you are gentlemen who will be content with what you find." The guests brought good bread, wine, and olives from the ship, along with the catch of the day, which, luckily, included an octopus. While the soup was heating, Telamon slapped the long tentacles against a rock by the stream to make them tender. Boiled and cut into bits, they were a great delicacy. It was a meal fit for the gods.

On the sixth day they saw on their right a low-lying plain, the district of Elis, and the shipmaster watched for the mouth of the river Peneos. There he would beach and unload the ship, the river being shallow at this time of summer. The men of Asini walked upstream to the town with their young athletes and did not leave them until they had found the gymnasium built of wood, simple and old, at the river's edge. Dion and Alexis gave their names, the name of their father, and of their town. They were not asked how old they were, since many of the contestants did not know the exact year of their birth. The judges separated the men from the boys by their physical maturity. From the moment when they were pronounced fit to compete, they were under the orders of the Olympic judges and their bodies were dedicated to Zeus.

Every house at Elis was open to the athletes as honored guests. The two from Asini asked for directions to the house of a man named Phineas, a friend of Aristes and a prosperous trader, who had a country retreat on the river, a mile from the gymnasium. Phineas was delighted to welcome the sons of his friend into his comfortable home. He gave them the best quarters and told his servants to make room among themselves for Telamon. Phineas kept pigs and goats, cows and horses. He said that athletes should eat meat every day, a rare luxury for the guests from Asini. After the evening meal that first night there was a comb of honey and a wicker basket of apples and peaches ripened in Phineas's own orchards.

They sat late while he talked about what they would be seeing in the coming month. Elis was not a walled city, but a scattering of houses and farms spread out along the river under a fortified hilltop. The town was quiet, only coming to life every four years when the athletes arrived from all over Greece to train for the Games. The gymnasium, a stadium, and, above all, a temple to Zeus, gave Elis its importance. It was the home of many Olympic victors and the priests of Elis controlled the Games at Olympia. It was they who prepared each athlete to compete in the Olympic spirit, first for the glory of the god; second, for the athlete's town; and only last, for himself. It was the priests who upheld the idea of excellence, reminding the contestants that the Games would prove their spirit and style as well as their skill. They must understand

31

that the winner of an event would be judged on many points, and all must abide by the judges' decisions without complaint.

"They have posted the names of the contestants for each event," Phineas said. "Alexis, I can tell you that there are a large number for the boys' race, as there always are. Usually they run in four or five heats and the winners run again for the final victory . . . but I suppose you know that. As for the boxers, only six names are entered this year. I know which one interests you, Dion. All of your father's friends are hoping you will be paired with Neleus's son Glaukon. But of course that is not decided until you go to Olympia. I assure you, I will be there to cheer for you."

He went on to describe the wonders of Olympia, the fertile valley with its plane trees and wild olives, the legendary river Alpheus, the nightingales, the sacred grove where the athletes would take their vows and offer sacrifices, the solemn moment when the priest ascended the steps of the great altar. They should see the green slopes of the stadium before the crowds trampled the grass. The hippodrome, close to the river, was the largest and finest in the world. Phineas himself had once ridden in an Olympic horse race there.

That night, for the first time, in the privacy of their room, Alexis and Dion carefully unwrapped Melissa's gifts for the gods. Alexis found a small statue, the figure of a young runner, his arms stretched forward, one foot pressed against the starting mark. Along the thigh, words were inscribed: *I belong to Zeus*. Dion's gift was a bronze dagger, very old, one of the treasures that Melissa had brought from Crete. On each side of the blade, finely worked in gold, were two bulls, their horns locked in combat.

The following day, Glaukon of Tiryns arrived in Elis

with his trainer. He had come over the mountains by chariot, bringing a servant to care for his clothing and do his cooking. His father had also sent four matched horses and a charioteer. The sight of such magnificence enraged Dion. At the same time, he was beginning to understand that he might never have a chance to fight against Glaukon.

"Like a fool, I never doubted that I would box with that devil from Tiryns," he said to Telamon. "Now it seems that the boxing matches are arranged by drawing lots at Olympia. Find some way to make sure that I am matched against Glaukon."

Wrapping Dion's hands for a practice bout, Telamon kept his voice low. "You give orders and I obey them, but I advise you to think carefully. Glaukon is now taller than you and outweighs you, or I miss my guess. They say that his trainer is well-known, even boasts to have trained several champion boxers in the new style."

"You speak the truth," Dion said shortly. "I give the orders and you obey them."

"In this new style, they win without striking a blow," urged Telamon. "They spar, dodge, keep out of reach, wear you out. That is not your way."

"No, it is not my way. I want to kill him."

"If you kill him, you forfeit the match."

"That is for the gods to decide. It is for you to make certain that I fight him."

Telamon shrugged skeptically and went off. He returned an hour later, but would say nothing until the brothers had finished training for the day and were well away from the gymnasium.

"What did you do?" Dion asked impatiently. "Were you able to arrange something?"

Telamon seldom gave simple answers. "Even the

33

stones have ears," he said. "This is a story that I heard today. There was a great man named Aristagorus, who was lord of Miletus under King Darius. He came to Sparta asking for help to throw off the yoke of Persia. The Spartan king, Cleomenes, refused. Again and again Aristagorus begged for help and Cleomenes refused. All this while, his little daughter was listening. Aristagorus began to offer money. Ten talents of gold . . . twenty talents . . . fifty. Then the little girl spoke. 'Father, you had better leave the room before this man reaches your price.' Every man has his price. Does that answer your question, Dion?"

No more was said on the subject until that night when Alexis spoke privately to Dion. "Telamon is an idiot. The last time he offered a bribe, he was sold into slavery. Still, it shows devotion."

Telamon's story was only one of many told about Sparta. The city was legendary in Asini, as it was in all of Greece. Men said that Sparta had no walls because it needed none, its highest class of citizens being soldiers who had no other duties. It was true that the Spartan system used slaves more brutally than other cities did, but the soldier aristocrats also lived like slaves. To harden their bodies they ate nothing but black bread and a vile kind of soup. They wore only one garment, winter and summer. If their sons were not born strong and likely to become soldiers, they were taken away as babies and exposed to die. Those who lived underwent tortures to prove their courage.

Alexis soon learned that there was a Spartan boy among the runners. He was a raw-boned young fellow, named Lampis after a famous Spartan athlete. Unsmiling and silent, he kept himself apart from the other athletes, except for a Spartan javelin thrower and one who was entering the pankration. The three could be seen talking together earnestly and solemnly in their free time, but these times were few. No other contestants were kept at work by their trainers so long or so hard as they were.

"That is the Spartan way," Telamon said, half admiring, half scornful. "Of course you must train to the limit of your ability, but they go beyond the limit. They say that all the rest of us are soft. Time will tell. All the same, Alexis, keep your eye on Lampis. You can be sure he has been doing nothing but train for the past year, and if he does not win the boys' race, he will hardly dare go home. He is the one to beat."

Telamon was also looking out for Dion's interests. One day they found him sitting in the doorway of Phineas's stable, at work on some strips of leather. "Try these," he said. He bound the new strips tightly and smoothly over Dion's knuckles. "I find that these are the kind the others will have. They are harder and thicker than the ones we have been using. From now on, I will do all I can to hurt you . . . to prepare for the real thing, you understand. Don't be drawn into a practice bout with anyone else. And of course, never mind trying to hurt *me*."

Elis was filled with athletes and trainers from even the farthest parts of Greece and from her colonies overseas. During the month of training they watched each other's habits and style. Alexis learned who paced himself well in trial runs and who was likely to burn out before the end of the stade, who waited until near the goal for a final burst of speed, and who tried to take the lead from the very start. The Spartan Lampis was one of these.

But even with such clues, no one could predict what would happen at Olympia. There, every runner would be making his maximum effort; here at Elis some might be making that effort in every race, while others might have reserves of strength and speed that they had not yet shown. Alexis himself did not know what he could do in Olympic competition. He had won easily in local festivals at Asini and at Nauplion, but Olympia was another matter.

Dion learned even less about the other boxers. Besides Glaukon, they came from Rhodes, famous for its boxers; from Astypalaea, a tiny Aegean island; and from Epidauros. The sixth man, Metrodorus of Athens, had already won the laurel wreath for a boxing match in the Pythian games at Delphi. He was the only one, except for Glaukon, in whom Dion expressed an interest. "When I have finished with Glaukon in the first bout, he will never fight again. Metrodorus will win his match, and if I am paired with him for the final bout, I will finish him." In the meantime boxers ran, shadowboxed, and sparred with their trainers, avoiding injuries. The final matches, as everyone knew, might stop just short of death.

Telamon mingled with the other trainers, relishing news and gossip from places he had known in his seafaring days. On the final day at Elis, he brought back to Phineas's house a piece of news that shook all but Dion, who was too much wrapped up in his coming match with Glaukon to understand or care what the story might mean. Telamon had met an athlete from Thessaly in the far north who said that King Darius had put his son-in-law, Mardonius, in command of a great army and many ships. Mardonius had led his army up the coast of Asia, driving out the Greek rulers of all the Ionian cities. He had then moved on north to the Hellespont, where the ships were waiting. According to the story, they had taken the northern island of Thasos without a struggle, enslaved the people, and sailed again westward to take cities on the mainland. This was all that the athlete from Thessaly knew, but it was happening perilously close to his home.

"Evidently Darius does not observe the Olympic truce," said Phineas, but his wry joke hardly dispelled the general gloom. Telamon raised his eyebrows to indicate that he had said all along what King Darius and his hordes of Persians would do.

However, even Telamon now had to put the Persian threat out of his mind. When morning dawned, the Olympic procession formed at Elis and began to move slowly down the sacred way.

· 2 ·

All day they moved southward between fields of wheat and flax where the harvest had been gathered. The athletes of each town marched together with horses and chariots, cheered on their way by a growing crowd who offered food and fresh water and wreaths of flowers. When night came, under a great golden moon now almost at the full, the marchers found shelters already set up for them in a grove of pine trees. Nothing was too good for the athletes.

At sunset on the second day they stopped at an altar on the boundary of Olympia. Here at the fountain of Piera, bubbling up clear and sparkling from some hidden spring that fed the sacred river Alpheus, the first rites of purification would take place. Alexis was dazed with expectation as he watched the leaders dipping their hands in the stream of water and drinking from it; first the judges in their purple robes, then the heralds of the truce, the umpires, and the trumpeters who would signal the start of the contests. The crowds along the road had now swelled to thousands, all intent on the ceremonies around the fountain, on the voice of the priest and the answering voices of the judges as they took their oaths. Smoke and flame rose from the altar. Then an upraised dagger flashed and descended. A sigh, as of satisfaction after tension, rippled through the crowd, and the blood of a young pig, the sacrificial animal, was poured out on the ground before the altar. Alexis prayed. If he won his race it could only be through the help of the god.

Now the athletes were moving forward again and Alexis caught sight of the men from Tiryns around a chariot with a tall young charioteer driving two black mares. Neleus was riding a third mare, and on the fourth rode Glaukon, handsome as a young god, his face calm and cheerful as he looked out over the crowd. Suddenly his expression changed as if he had caught sight of someone he knew, and, looking where Glaukon looked, Alexis saw his own father with Niki at his side. Now that the sacrifice had ended, Aristes was trying to get to the edge of the road, his face glowing with pride, his eyes fixed on his sons. Niki was on tiptoe, staring straight at Glaukon as if she were looking at Heracles himself. "You see it too," Dion muttered to Alexis. "Well, I will put an end to it."

They saw Gorgo pulling Niki away. Then, as the procession disbanded, familiar faces from home surrounded Aristes and his sons. The men of Asini who had brought them to Elis a month ago had come again with Aristes to man his ship and to cheer for their town. They crowded forward to the road and led the way to a tent set up near the entrance to the sacred grove, the Altis, where the opening ceremonies would take place the following day.

Aristes dismissed the Asinians with warm thanks for

the comfortable pallets they had made ready. "Our friends have done well for us," he said. "And they have put Niki and Gorgo in an excellent spot to the south of the river with the other women." He laughed. "They are near the booths, in the midst of all the hubbub. Sweetmeats, tumblers, music . . . Niki could ask for nothing more."

In the morning he brought out new linen tunics, made on Melissa's looms, dyed a deep blue and bordered with gold thread in a pattern of tridents that she herself had woven. Aristes said that the color and design were her own idea, and Gorgo told him privately that Melissa had sold a pair of her earrings to buy the gold thread. The tunics and their wearers drew admiring looks from the crowd.

Afterward, Alexis could not remember all that had happened at Olympia. It was as if he had been thrown into a whirlpool; the crowds, the herds of animals penned up for the sacrifices, the wine merchants and fruit vendors, singers and acrobats, poets and soothsayers—all left little impression.

Some things he did not want to remember, but some of the best were never to be forgotten—how he had waked at night and heard the nightingales, how the athletes had entered the Altis for the first time.

They went in by way of a straight path that led from the northern to the southern limit of the sacred grounds, and gathered, a great throng with their fathers, brothers, and trainers, to speak their vows at the steps of the Council House. Alexis was prepared for this; it had been described to the athletes at Elis a month ago. Within the Council House walls, as everyone knew, was a great statue, Zeus of the Oaths, holding a thunderbolt in each hand. In front of the statue on this solemn morning a boar had been sacrificed and burned. But Alexis was not prepared for the awe he felt as he stood in the silent crowd, waiting for the arrival of the priest who would bring out the ashes of the sacrifice.

Now he was coming. He stood on the steps of the Council House, an old man, but tall and straight, wearing a white robe, beautifully and precisely draped. Above his head he raised an urn. All could see, and his warning rang out, easily reaching the farthest edges of the crowd. If any man there was guilty of crimes of blood, or of sacrilege toward the gods, that man should leave. If there were any women present, they should leave. When no one moved, he administered the first oath and the athletes repeated the words after him: "I swear that I am a free-born Greek; my fathers before me were free-born Greeks." Then came the Olympic oath. Alexis's voice was lost, even to his own ears, in a great wave of sound drowning all other sound as the athletes responded: "I swear that I have given ten months of my utmost strength in mind and body to prepare for this day. I will obey the rules. I will accept no bribes." Alexis, looking beyond the walls of the Council House, saw the holy river flowing through the fertile valley, and the rim of dark mountains touching the sky. He felt the presence of the god and his knees trembled. It was as if almighty Zeus held them all in the hollow of his hand.

In the afternoon Dion went off to the eastern edge of the Altis where there were practice grounds for boxing, wrestling, and the pankration, that most violent of all Olympic events. Meanwhile, in stables near the hippodrome, drivers and owners were examining horses' hoofs and the yokes and wheels of chariots. This year the equestrian events would open the Games on the second day.

Alexis joined other athletes who were gathering in the stadium. It all looked just as he had been told. The stadium was six hundred feet long, and wide enough for twenty runners to compete. On both sides, the green slopes were already filled with spectators watching favorite sons in a last practice, anxiously noting the competition, and laying bets. Alexis ran a length of the stadium, the length that he knew well from practice on the beach at home, yet here so different in every other way. The crowds, the heat, the dust made him feel tense and tired. He was running badly. Every other boy was running better than he. His spirits were low when he returned to the tent. Dion, on the contrary, was cheerful, knowing that he was in top form and condition.

Sooner or later everyone came to Olympia, and on the second day there was a crowd of twenty thousand. No one wanted to miss the chariot race, the most beautiful and the most dangerous of all Olympic events. The slopes around the hippodrome were already so packed that Alexis could only shoulder his way forward for a glimpse of the starting gates, but even a glimpse was worth the effort. The gilded chariots were ranged like the great golden arrowhead of some god.

Behind the gate nearest to him was the chariot from Tiryns. The tall young charioteer stood tense but held the reins lightly, waiting for the sound of the trumpet that would signal the drop of the gates. Alexis saw that he had tied the ends of the reins around his waist. There were a dozen other chariots, each with four horses, some quiet under the hands of their grooms, some trampling the dust nervously. The trumpet sounded. The gates were dropping two by two, those farthest back at the outer edges of the course moving first. It was a fair start. Now all of the chariots were in line and off down the track with a thunder of hoofs and a cloud of dust. Alexis saw no more.

The shouts of the charioteers and even the din of rattling chariot wheels were lost in the roar of the crowd. A big man at Alexis's elbow was bawling, "They're at the turn!" He hoisted Alexis to his shoulders for a brief sight of wheels and whips and horses bunched at the far end of the course. They were swerving violently for the turn around the post. Then came the sound of a crash, of another, and a third. The big man jerked Alexis from his shoulders and plunged away. As the crowd surged forward and then back again, Alexis found himself in front, pressed against the barrier, with a clear view of what had happened. The whole field seemed filled with the wrecks of chariots that had collided at the turning post. Then he saw the chariot from Tiryns passing around the wreckage with a free course before it. The black mares were at full gallop, their breath throwing off spume, their manes flying. Suddenly another chariot drew even with them. Above the uproar Alexis heard shouts and screams: "Athens! Athens! . . . Tiryns!" He looked up, praying, "Father Zeus, send an omen." Far above in the sky, a bird floated motionless on some current of air. Was it an eagle of Zeus? Was it on his right, as a sign of answered prayer?

The two teams were rounding the post at the near end of the course. They had cleared it and, neck and neck, rounded the far post again, first one and then the other pulling ahead as they came down the race course. The black mares reached the near post and Alexis saw the charioteer slacken his left rein to make the turn. Then he saw the chariot jolt as a wheel struck the edge of the post. Suddenly the axle splintered and the chariot was turning end over end. The black mares galloped on, their driver held by the reins tied around his waist. The crowd screamed out in pity as he was dragged down the whole length of the race course. Only at the far end were the grooms able to catch the horses and cut loose the body of the charioteer.

Alexis found his father and Dion. Together, without a word, they left the race course. Alexis's mind was in turmoil. He had prayed for an omen and immediately the accident had happened. Was he then responsible for the death of the young charioteer, who was from Tiryns but a total stranger to him? He should be feeling satisfaction, and instead he felt pity. He did not dare to tell this to his father or to Dion; but to Telamon, in private, he could say anything.

"An omen?" said Telamon with a short laugh. "Who knows? I wonder if Neleus remembers Aesop's fable about the eagle. Last night while you were in the Altis, I was listening to a poet. He was attracting a good crowd and had, in fact, put that very fable into verse:

> *An eagle, struck by an arrow from a bow,*
> *Said, when he saw the winged traitor,*
> *'So, not by others but by our own plumes*
> *We're taken.'*

"Not bad, is it? His name is Aeschylus. If you run across him, listen. You might learn something."

"Don't talk in riddles," Alexis said fretfully.

"In simple language, my child, Neleus is a rich man. He entered his chariot in a rich man's sport, a dangerous one. His charioteer made a mistake. That is all you need to know. Besides, this is no time to upset yourself. Remember, you race first thing tomorrow morning. Find a quiet road and have a good run. There's nothing like it for putting the mind at rest.

"You have already missed the races on horseback," he

43

added. "You might do well to miss the pentathlon, too. It goes on all afternoon and the stadium will be damnably hot. But meet me there when the pentathlon is over. I will be working with Dion and you should try the race course to get the feel of it."

Alexis took Telamon's advice and found that an easy run on a shady road did clear his mind of confusion, while the trial sprint at the stadium focused his will on tomorrow's race.

In the evening when he had joined his father and Dion in their tent, Niki appeared with Gorgo. Niki's eyes were bright, her color high with excitement. The old nurse looked harried and angry.

"Sir, please speak to your daughter," she said to Aristes. "Twice she has got away from me and been gone for hours. When I ask where she has been, she makes no sense. I can't be responsible for her if she behaves like this."

"Don't scold me, father," begged Niki, smiling. "Gorgo is so slow, and I wanted to see everything, you know. You aren't annoyed with me, are you?"

Aristes frowned and seemed about to speak harshly to her for once, but she disarmed him. "Today I was going to buy a necklace for myself. Then I saw a fortuneteller with a coop full of chickens, and I spent the money to get a good omen for all of you—because I love you." She looked at each of them with irresistible appeal.

Her father relented and only said teasingly, "You must stay with Gorgo, my little one, no matter how slow she may be. But now, since you were so generous with my money, what did the fortuneteller say?"

"Oh, you know how they are. They never have anything really good to say. It doesn't mean anything to me:

'What we look for does not come to pass;
The god finds a way that we did not expect.' "

Aristes laughed and ruffled her cropped hair. "An old
saying. I could have told you that without consulting the
insides of a chicken."

"But I have made sure that my brothers will win," she
said. "There are so many altars to Artemis here that I
thought it must be a sign. I offered my old doll at one of
her altars and the priest accepted it. Most of the people
who look at me think I'm a boy because of my hair, but he
knew I wasn't and he smiled and said that the goddess
would be pleased. So, you see, Alexis, now I have even
parted with my doll. It means that I have grown up." Suddenly there were tears in her eyes and she ran off, Gorgo
following as best she could.

When they had gone, Telamon asked, "Have you
chosen an altar for your offerings?" And when the brothers
confessed that they had not done so, he said, "Look for the
statue of Zeus, the Bringer of Fate. It is in the hippodrome
near the starting point for the chariot race. It would not be
a bad choice, win or lose."

They found the statue easily. It was carved of dark
wood and very old, judging by its stiff pose and its up-
turned, mysterious smile. Several other athletes were there
before them and an attendant stood nearby, adding olive
twigs to a fire that burned on a low altar. When he had
fed their sacrifices of incense and honey cakes to the flames
and poured out a libation of wine on the earth, he accepted
the sword and the little statue of the runner and set them
carefully among the offerings at the foot of the altar.

That night the full moon rose. Pale gold, it shone
bright on Olympia, casting black shadows among temples

45

and statues, lighting the faces of those who had won and those who had lost. All night Alexis could hear shouts and laughter above the sound of flute and lyre. Later, the nightingales sang, piercingly loud and sweet. Lying in the tent, he knew that he should be sleeping, but that was impossible. How absurd that he, Alexis of Asini, a small town too poor to have a first-rate trainer, should compete with runners from Athens and Corinth, from Thebes and Rhodes—and above all with Lampis, the boy from Sparta. Runners from all of these famous cities must have had skillful training. Surely they had not been told to teach themselves to run. He would not be good enough. He would make a fool of himself. Why was he not at home in bed where life was familiar and easy? Alexis was sure that he had not slept all night long when he felt Telamon shaking his shoulder. The night was over, the morning star was in the sky, and the day of the race had come.

In the first light the athletes came again to the Altis and gathered around the altar of Zeus at the center of the sacred olive grove. It towered high, filled with the ashes of sacrifices offered for more years than any living man could remember or even guess. A priest moved through the crowd, carrying a torch from the eternal fire that burned on the altar of Hestia, goddess of the hearth. He climbed the steps to the top of the altar of Zeus and set fire to the wood piled there. The smell of blazing poplar and of incense filled the grove. Then the Olympic flame burst through the smoke and the crowd gave a sigh like the sound of a wave breaking on a long beach. Officials were coming with this year's sacrifices for the Games, baskets of meat cut from the thighs of a hundred cattle that had been brought to the slaughter with their horns gilded and with wreaths of flowers about their necks. At last the fire died down and was quenched with water from the Alpheus. When the ashes were cold, they would be hard and smooth, and the altar of Zeus would have mounted even closer to heaven; earth, air, fire, and water mingled to praise him who ruled all things. On the last night of the Games, after the gods were satisfied, the crowds would feast.

Alexis remembered what followed as if it had been a dream. Somehow he got to the stadium for the boys' race. The slopes were filling, many of last night's revelers having stretched out to sleep there. Alexis drew his lot. Luckily, he was to run in the first heat and would have time to rest while four other heats were run, supposing that he survived to run in the finals. There were fifteen boys in the first heat, but Lampis was not among them.

He remembered very little from the moment he toed the starting line and heard the trumpet until he reached the finish. He only knew that another runner had been ahead of him almost to the end. Then, with the blood beating in his ears and his lungs bursting, he had somehow closed the gap. But he did not know that he had won until he fell into the crowd at the finish line and felt himself being pounded on the back to shouts of "Asini! Asini has won the first heat! Alexis of Asini!"

His mouth was dry, his head throbbing. Then his father and Dion were breaking a path for him through the crowd to a stone water basin where he took a long drink and sank down on the grass. He could not believe that he had won. His legs were numb. Could he run again? He needed time, and it would not take much time to run off four more heats.

Telamon was rubbing him down and gently kneading the muscles of his legs. "There will be time enough. The

47

managers will be announcing the name and town of each contestant, you know, and the umpires usually argue about who has won, and there may be some false starts. It all takes time. You will be ready."

It was as Telamon had predicted. Twice the heats were delayed when runners made false starts and were punished by sharp blows from officials with long forked sticks. But Lampis won his heat easily, and all too soon they were announcing the final race for boys.

Aristes and Dion embraced Alexis. Above the noise of the crowd he could not hear what they were saying— something about Lampis, something about Asini—but he knew what they meant, and nodded as he went to the starting line.

"Eucles of Athens . . ." All over the stadium Athenians shouted encouragement to their runner. "Sotades of Elis . . . Lampis of Sparta . . . Alexis of Asini . . . Troilus of Delphi . . ." Each name was followed by cheers from some parts of the stadium and silence from others whose own champions had been beaten by one of the finalists or whose own city had been at war with one of these cities.

Alexis stared down the length of the stadium to the finish line. Lampis was the one to beat and he had to do it for Asini. But Lampis always went into the lead from the very start. If Alexis held himself back this time, tired as he was, he would never be able to close the gap at the end. He must start fast and stay even with Lampis all the way, then do even better in the last stretch. He drew a deep breath, let it out, and leaned forward, his toes gripping the starting stone. The trumpet blared and the runners shot forward.

Out of the corner of his eye Alexis saw to his left Lampis and the boy from Elis, running smoothly. On his right, no one. Athens and Delphi were somewhere behind.

Another glance showed him that Lampis was going into the lead. Alexis felt his lungs and his legs laboring painfully. Then suddenly he heard, as if the words were spoken, "I belong to Zeus." He saw in his mind the beach at Asini, and he felt his breath coming easily and powerfully. His leg muscles were obeying his will and he was overtaking, passing Lampis. The crowd at the finish line loomed up and overwhelmed him.

It was over. Alexis had won. Sprays of flowers and olive branches flicked his shoulders. Arms pummeled him. And then, while faces were still a blur, he saw one familiar face that made him think he had gone mad. It happened in a flash. Slender arms were around his neck and a girl's voice spoke into his ear. "You won and I saw you win! Oh, you are excellent!"

It was Niki. Niki where no girl was allowed to be on pain of death, Niki with her hair cropped so like a boy's and wearing one of his old tunics that she must have brought from home, planning this trick all along. No one seemed to be giving her even a second glance, but his blood froze.

"You fool!" he said under his breath. "Quick! Leave, before it's too late. You know the penalty."

"I don't believe in the penalty." She gave him a flashing smile and slipped away into the crowd.

Telamon was wiping the sweat from Alexis's face, his father and brother lifted him shoulder-high, and his townsmen put a crown of flowers on his head. They tied a ribbon on his arm, another on his thigh, and so carried him to the stone seat of the judges to receive the palm branch that would serve as a token of victory until the final night when victors were crowned with wild olive. As Alexis looked down, dazed and smiling, from his high perch, he saw Lampis, his cheeks white and tear-stained, leaving the

49

crowd, followed by his grim-faced trainer. Again, in the midst of his own triumph, Alexis felt pity. It was a weakness, one he must try to overcome. He did not allow himself to picture the arrival of Lampis in Sparta.

But the men of Asini would remember Alexis's victory only as the prelude to what they felt the next day as they waited for Dion to box against Glaukon of Tiryns, for the lots fell as Telamon had promised.

The contestants were not matched according to experience or weight, but by small wooden tokens marked in pairs and drawn from a silver urn. The choice was therefore on the knees of the gods. Under the scrutiny of an official, each boxer drew out his token without looking at it. A second official took it from him and handed it to a third, who announced the letter marked on the token. "Beta . . . gamma . . . alpha . . ." Who could tamper with such a system? Yet Telamon had found a way. "Dion, son of Aristes, of Asini—beta . . . Glaukon, son of Neleus, of Tiryns—beta."

As an Olympic victor and brother of a contestant, Alexis stood with his father and their townsmen in places at the front. Dion and Glaukon would be the second pair to fight.

The first match was over almost as soon as it began. The winner was a burly man, Cleomedes of Astypalaea, no longer young, his nose flattened, his ears crumpled from many bouts. Within his beard his open mouth showed broken teeth. But he had the neck muscles of a bull and his eyes glared under his heavy brows. His massive shoulders and long arms delivered a barrage of deadly blows into the face and about the head of his opponent, a younger man in his first Olympic match, Iccus of Epidauros, who could not return blow for blow. Suddenly Alexis saw Cleomedes's arm reach out and catch Iccus's arm. Then came a crushing blow to the jaw. Iccus's head jerked sharply to one side, and back; he dropped to the dust and lay still, his face covered with blood. The shouting died, followed by cries of "Foul! Holding!" and the sound of the crowd muttering uneasily. There had been too much blood and the match had been too uneven.

While his trainer and some of his townsmen carried Iccus out of the stadium, the big man walked to the judges' platform and received his palm branch, but the applause was scattered and half-hearted. Alexis felt sick as he watched Telamon winding the leather thongs about Dion's hands. Already, faces were turning again to the cleared ground in the center of the stadium. The crowd wanted to forget the distasteful spectacle of the first match and looked forward to a better fight, knowing that the next two opponents were more evenly paired. Glaukon was somewhat taller and heavier, but both were young and fighting their first Olympic match.

Cleomedes, waving his palm branch and grinning, had not yet left the stadium when Alexis saw a man coming from the direction of the dressing rooms. He pushed through to the judges' seats and there was an agitated consultation. Then one of the judges stepped forward and his voice carried over the silent crowd. "Iccus of Epidauros has died of injuries inflicted by Cleomedes. Cleomedes forfeits the match."

Like an animal at bay, Cleomedes looked about him, seeming bewildered by the jeers and insults hurled at him from all sides. He laid his palm branch on the judges' table, then went off toward the dressing rooms, mumbling to himself and shaking his head repeatedly, as if to clear it.

The trumpets blew. The chief official announced the

51

names of the next contestants and exhorted them to do their best for the glory of their cities, for the joy of their fathers, and for their own good names. Dion and Glaukon took their stance at close range, the left shoulder and fist on guard, the right fist ready to jab. Alexis saw that his brother's face was set in a look of cold hatred. Glaukon's expression he could not judge, but he appeared calm and alert.

An umpire raised his staff, then lowered it. Dion struck the first blow, a right to the ear, and followed it with a left to the chin, but Glaukon parried and dodged, making no effort to return the blows. His footwork was agile, exact. Time after time Dion struck, and Glaukon was still unmarked.

"He is a stylist," Aristes said scornfully. "I know that sort. They expect to win by technique alone. But watch. My son will outlast him and outbox him, too."

The fight continued while the midday sun beat mercilessly down on the two men in the center of the stadium, and Aristes's confidence gradually changed to a furious despair. A rest was permitted if a boxer asked for it by going down on one knee, but neither Glaukon nor Dion would admit to fatigue. Some of the spectators were leaving, overcome with the intense heat or with boredom, but those from Asini watched, stupified, unable to help Dion in any way, and sure that he would drop dead of exhaustion.

At last the official stepped between the contestants, calling out, "I order a climax. Each of you, in turn, will strike an undefended blow until there is a winner. The first blow will be decided by the toss of a coin." The two boxers made their choice, and the coin fell in the dust.

"Heads! Dion of Asini will strike the first blow."

Again the two faced one another at close range.

Glaukon took a defensive stance, but his hands hung loose, almost at his sides as he waited for the blow. Dion, on the offense, drew back his open right hand and swung with all his remaining strength. The edge of his hand chopped with stunning force under Glaukon's jaw. Glaukon toppled and fell. Then, as shouts mounted to a roar, he staggered to his feet. Dion braced himself, his head down, his left foot advanced, the knees flexed to take whatever might come. Now, for the first time, Glaukon struck hard. It was an upward blow into the face. Dion dropped to his hands and knees, his head almost in the dust.

Alexis heard his father's hoarse shout. "Get up! You can still beat him!" Then, with a stifled groan, "No . . . No. Enough is enough."

Even as Aristes spoke, Dion had raised his head. He pushed himself to his feet and the crowd went mad with excitement. But the judges were consulting, and before either fighter could prepare for the next blow, the official with the wand silenced the frenzied shouting with a gesture and the decision. "I declare the match a draw."

Dion and Glaukon stared dully at one another. Glaukon seemed about to speak, even to hold out his hand, but Dion did not respond. They turned away to receive their palm branches and to fall into the arms of their friends. The coveted olive crown would be given to neither but would be dedicated to Zeus.

The last match was excellent and hard fought, Metrodorus of Athens being a clear winner over the boxer from Rhodes.

On the fifth night at Olympia, the victors received their crowns of wild olive in the sacred grove, standing at a marble table, richly carved. That same night there was wonderful news that spread like wildfire. Phineas of Elis brought it to Alexis when he came, among the first, to congratulate him. King Darius's fleet had been wrecked in a storm. Rounding the promontory of Mt. Athos as they were heading south to attack Athens, many of the ships had been sunk by fierce waves and others dashed against the rocks. Only a remnant had survived to turn back toward the coast of Asia. "And I am the happiest of men," Phineas concluded. "Elis won the race in armor and the pankration, and I had the honor of entertaining the glorious sons of my friend Aristes."

But on the return voyage, Aristes expressed the dissatisfaction felt by all the men from Asini. "If there were any justice, Dion would have won the crown. See how it fell out. Cleomedes won easily, but he was disqualified. They called Dion's match a draw, though we all saw that he was the better man. And the Athenian won the crown without fighting a second match."

In the shadow of the sail, Dion lay silent, an arm across his face.

"Some god was behind it," Telamon said gloomily. "When the Immortals do mischief, man is helpless. But Dion should have had a better trainer. I only know the old way of boxing, where honest blows count, not dancing about. Well, I will soon be gone. Find him a new trainer, someone like that man from Tiryns. Dion can box again at Olympia. There is always another wreath to win."

Niki sat on the deck of the ship, gazing across the water, her arms about her knees. "Do you know what I did at Olympia?" she said, looking at her father. "No, don't frown. Gorgo was with me. Yesterday when the Games had finished and women could go to the stadium, I found the altar to Demeter, across from the judges' stand. Did you see it? The statue looks sad, I think, but kind, like Melissa.

A girl is standing with her . . . Persephone, I suppose. She looks gentle. I had nothing to give but a wreath of flowers, so I gave that, and the priestess accepted it. I asked the goddess to take care of all of us."

"And what did the priestess tell you?" Aristes asked, smiling.

"She only said that Demeter knows the future of our life and death but cannot change it. So I think, Father . . . I think we had better take care of ourselves. And I hope that Dion will not fight again with Glaukon."

Dion sat up. "Be quiet, Niki. I will fight him again, and soon."

"By the way," Alexis asked Telamon, "how did you arrange the match?"

"It was very simple," said Telamon. "The athletes do not look at the lots they have drawn. Neither does the first official, nor the second, if you remember. Only the third official sees which letters are written on the tokens. He was the only man I had to deal with. And as luck would have it, he came from Samos. No, you owe me nothing, Aristes. I gave him no money. I merely offered to recommend him to my father for any help he may need when he returns to his business affairs in Samos."

There was a general laugh of grudging admiration. Only Dion was silent. He moved back into the shadow of the sail, muttering, "The sun hurts my eyes." He threw his cloak over his head and avoided the light as much as possible for the rest of the voyage.

The closer they came to Asini, the more Alexis thought about Melissa. He felt sure that her gift, the little statue of the runner, had helped him to win his race. "I belong to Zeus." Melissa would be glad when he told her how the words had come to him when he needed them.

On the last day of the voyage, sitting in the prow of the vessel with Niki, Alexis told her what had happened.

"That will make her smile," Niki said. "She is beautiful when she smiles."

"Then why should she ever look sad?" he wondered aloud.

"Don't you know why?"

When he shook his head, she spoke into his ear. "Melissa loves our father. Not like a wife. I mean, she is in love with him."

Alexis stared at her. "How do you know?"

"I can see it. And he doesn't love her. Not that way."

"He treats her well," Alexis protested.

"Of course." She gave a little shrug and said no more.

Alexis was disturbed, not only because of what Niki had told him but because she seemed to know so much about love. He remembered too well how she had looked at Glaukon. What had she been doing when she slipped away from Gorgo at Olympia? Had she seen Glaukon privately? He knew that he should ask her outright, but could not do it.

He delayed telling Dion about the conversation because his brother did not want to talk to anyone. Before they reached Asini everyone knew why. Dion told his father that he was losing the sight in his left eye.

"It will heal," Aristes said confidently. "All you need is a few days rest, never fear."

· III ·

To Epidauros

·1·

NEWS of Alexis's victory had already reached Asini, brought by travelers who had crossed quickly from Olympia over the mountain roads. A watchman on the tower sighted the ship long before it rounded the promontory, and when the voyagers dropped anchor, the beach was full of their townspeople. They knew every detail of Dion's fight, too, and judged him to be a victor unfairly cheated of his crown. A crowd of men waded out to carry Aristes and his glorious sons to shore.

Among all the smiling faces, Alexis could not find the one he wanted most to see. Melissa was not there. He saw his grandmother drawing his father aside, out of the crowd, and speaking urgently. Then Aristes disappeared quickly through the gate that led upward to the palace.

Alexis pushed his way to Chrysis. "What is it? What has happened?"

The old woman patted his hand. "Melissa . . ." Then looking into his stricken face, "No, no, nothing serious. She will recover, but the child was born too soon and too weak to live . . . a girl. We did all we could to save her. It was an unlucky time, or perhaps some god was angry."

Perhaps some god was angry. First the injury to Dion's eye, and now the loss of Melissa's child. To Alexis it was a clear sign that he must plan revenge against Glaukon at once and carry out the plan alone. Sooner or later Aristes would surely wreak vengeance on the father. It was for Alexis to destroy the son. He told no one his thoughts, but Niki, always responsive to his moods, seemed subdued and anxious, her usually bright spirit clouded. Once she spoke of Tiryns, as if inviting him to speak his mind about Glaukon. He made no answer. It was better to act than to talk.

When Melissa was able to leave her bed, she took up her household duties as before. Alexis saw that she was pale and looked older, but she did not speak about the baby. It was Chrysis who told all that there was to tell. "Melissa had made a doll for the baby and we laid it with the child in a grave by Abas's grave on the cliff. Do not grieve, Alexis. Your little sister is with Persephone. She is a kind goddess, you know, and she will play with the child as a mother would do. But Melissa's heart is broken. She had such a great hope."

At the end of a week, Melissa still had no strength, and Gorgo advised her to bathe in the fountain where the goddess Hera went every year to renew her youth. The fountain was nearby in a valley behind their own hills, and as the weather was still warm and dry, Melissa was persuaded to make the journey. Aristes ordered a litter for her comfort, and an armed guard of servants surrounded her, Gorgo following on foot with gifts for the goddess.

When they returned the following day, Gorgo insisted that Melissa was cured, but Melissa only said with a faint smile, "I bathed in the fountain and did all they told me to do. The priestess gave me herbs steeped in wine. But the water was very cold and the wine was no different from what you give me, Chrysis. I feel the same as before."

Soon afterward, Aristes's artist freeman finished carving the monument for Abas's grave and the family went to inspect the work. At Telamon's urging even Dion came, leaving the dark room where he spent his days. The stone pillar stood at the head of Abas's grave with the small grave next to it, and coming closer they saw the carving. In bold relief it showed a snake curled around the trunk of an apple tree.

Niki shivered. "I do not like the snake. There are real snakes here on the cliff when the sun warms the rocks. I have seen them and they frighten me."

"You are a foolish girl, Niki," said Chrysis. "Don't you know what the artist meant? That is the serpent who guards the golden apples on the tree of eternal life. You have seen serpents shed their skins. That too means eternal life. It is why they guard our graves. The serpent is wise and gives healing. If you see one, remember that it may be a god, or it may be the soul of a loved one. Come here often, and when you come, bring a bowl of milk and some honey cakes. If a serpent accepts your offering, it is an honor to you."

Her old eyes narrowed as she studied the carving again. "Melissa, you should go to Epidauros. You and Dion should go together. The serpent god might heal both of you."

The serpent . . . healing. Alexis remembered a doctor at Nauplion who kept a snake in a basket. When they returned to the palace, he mentioned it to Telamon, who shook his head. "Every doctor has a snake. That does not mean that all doctors can heal. Chrysis is right. Melissa and Dion should go to Epidauros. There the healing god is truly present. To human eyes he appears as a snake, but only his priestess sees him. He is kept underground."

Aristes overheard and frowned. A mere handful of coins lay between this slave and freedom, and already he was behaving like a free man, free to give advice even to the master. Nevertheless Aristes looked thoughtful. An ailing wife and son were of little use or pleasure to him, and Epidauros might be the best hope of a quick cure for both.

Epidauros, a day's easy journey east of Asini, was the most famous of many shrines to Asklepios, the healing god, son of Apollo. Other gods too could heal, but none like Asklepios. His divine father had chosen a mortal maiden to be the mother, and she had given birth to the radiant child in a hillside cave at Epidauros. The power of the god worked through the compassionate son, who loved mankind. Asklepios could heal any kind of disease and would have raised the dead if Zeus had not forbidden it. Pure, immaculate, full of harmony and truth, Asklepios healed both body and mind by putting them in tune with the divine laws that made the universe give out its glorious harmonies.

The next day, Aristes arranged for Melissa to go to Epidauros. When she asked how long she must stay away from home, he answered that she must stay as long as necessary. She must not worry about the household. It was high time for Niki to make herself useful and learn how to direct the servants.

Dion could not be persuaded to go and it was of no use to force him when he had no faith, but Telamon said, "You are like your grandfather's lyre, silent, out of tune, useless. Remember the lessons I used to give you? Harmony, and the divine laws of nature—have you forgotten all of that? Apollo's lyre? At Epidauros you will remember what I said, and you will understand it at last."

"I am not going," Dion said sullenly. "My eye is already better. Besides, Epidauros is for women and children and weaklings who will believe any nonsense."

"The gods do answer prayers," said Alexis. He told Dion how in his race he had heard the words "I belong to Zeus" and felt the surge of some power beyond himself that had sped him on to victory.

"You were getting your second wind," Dion scoffed.

"No, listen to me," Alexis said. "In the chariot race I prayed. I did not pray that the charioteer from Tiryns would be killed, but he was killed. Doesn't that mean that the gods are listening? Doesn't it mean that our revenge has begun? The gods do hear us, Dion. Go to Epidauros. They say the power of Asklepios is very great. Surely he can heal you."

Dion would not be persuaded and even Melissa sounded reluctant. "Your father will get in the grape harvest," she said to Niki, "and then he will have a cargo for Crete. He will be thinking of a thousand things. But for me at Epidauros the time will seem long."

"Of course the time will seem long to her," Niki told Alexis. "She will think only about our father. Alexis, ask him to let you go to Epidauros with Melissa. I will take care of the house, and Dion could help in the vineyards, if he would. Our father is too kind. He should order Dion out of that dark room and make him work."

In the end, Niki arranged everything. On the first day of the grape harvest, Dion went off to the vineyards with his father, and Alexis left for Epidauros with Melissa, riding with the guard and keeping a sharp watch for any danger. A lady, carried in a litter and obviously from a great house, could be a tempting prey for roving bandits in this part of the Peloponnese. The donkey that carried

Gorgo also carried food and valuable gifts for the shrines of Apollo and Asklepios at Epidauros. However, no threat appeared.

It was a journey of about twenty miles. They passed the home farms and their barns full of harvested grain. Then the road led eastward among isolated upland farms where men were at work in their grape arbors and great baskets brimmed with the vintage. After the last of the farms the travelers were among the mountains. In the warm sunshine the air was still and sweet with roadside lavender and thyme. There was no sound but the hum of bees and now and then the thin clear piping of a shepherd high above them.

At day's end, their shadows moving before them in the light of the setting sun, they came down into an open valley. The road led through cool groves of pine trees, then narrowed into a path. In simple shelters under the trees, people were cooking an evening meal. The path ended at a high wooden archway carved with twining serpents and the words, *He who would enter here must think as the god thinks.*

Beyond, half hidden by trees and shrubs, lay some wooden houses, thatched with reed, and from one of these a young priest came to meet them. Courteously he asked who they were and what was wanted. When he heard Alexis's name he knew him at once as an Olympic winner and bowed with grave respect. Then he put aside the curtains of the litter and spoke a brief greeting to Melissa. He gave his own name as Peteos.

"You and your men will find food and beds in the shelters," he said to Alexis. "Tomorrow they can return home. The lady will be safe here. She will sleep in the abaton with her servant, and you will see her every day."

Telling the litter bearers to follow him, he went off toward a long building at the far end of the sanctuary. Alexis saw the door opening. Melissa entered, and the door closed behind her.

He did not see her again until the next evening when she came down from the mountain shrine of Apollo, high above Epidauros, where the first sacrifice was always made. She came to meet him outside the gateway and they sat together on a bench under a pine tree. In the warmth, the pine needles sent up their spicy fragrance. A copper-colored snake lay sunning itself on a stone.

"Gorgo did well to bring a cock for the sacrifice," Melissa said cheerfully. Her face shone with faith and hope. "The priest said that Apollo was pleased with the gifts of all who came today, even the poor who had nothing to give but their prayers. He told us to pray with clean hands and a pure heart, asking for whatever is best for us, whether or not we know what it is. And he told us not to fear the serpents here. They belong to Asklepios and are harmless. I felt the presence of the god."

"I felt it too," said Alexis. "I spent the day walking about with the young priest who met us yesterday. I talked to others too who are learning to be healers—Asklepiads they are called—and they tell about wonderful cures. Many women come here to pray for the birth of children, and many come to be healed of blindness. If only Dion would come . . ."

"But he need not come," said Melissa. She spoke with an enthusiasm that he had never heard in her voice. "You could do it all for him. I talked to a woman who slept next to me in the abaton last night. We talked as friends. She came here in place of her daughter, who is barren and wants a child. The mother bathed in the sacred fountain of

Epidauros as I did. She too fasted, and went up the mountain to Apollo's shrine. And each day she will talk to a priest, as I will do. When the right time comes, the priest gives a cup of wine mixed with bitter herbs. Then you sleep, and the god comes to you in a dream. When you wake, a priest tells you the meaning of your dream and you know what you must do to be cured. Sometimes you wake already cured. My friend's daughter will be healed, even though she lives far away. She will bear a child. You can do these things for Dion, and he will be healed."

"I will try," he said. "I would do anything if Dion could be as he was, with two good eyes, able to go again to Olympia and this time win a crown. I will make an olive wreath for an offering, like an Olympic wreath."

In the morning, accompanied by Peteos, Alexis passed under the archway into the sanctuary and found Melissa waiting. She said that she had not slept so well since her girlhood. They went first to the temple of Asklepios, still standing from the ancient days, its roof raised on pillars of sweet-smelling cedar wood that cast their long shadows on the floor of well-swept earth. In a patch of sunlight stood the statue of Asklepios leaning on a staff. It had been carved so long ago that the stone was crumbling, but the face looked kind and the mouth seemed open, as if about to speak. One could still see the serpent winding about the staff.

"That is he," said Peteos. He stood, his hands lightly clasped, looking up into the face of the god. "It is how we think of him, wise, able to heal in the way he knows is best. But it is only a statue. Come, and I will show you where the god himself lives."

At the far end of the temple, behind the statue, earth had been formed into a smooth mound more than head-high. A passageway into one side of the mound led to a heavy door. As they approached this door, Melissa's fingers touched Alexis's arm, trembling. The voice of the priest changed as if he had removed himself to another world. "This is the tomb of Asklepios. Within is the labyrinth where the god was buried. His body has returned to dust, but his spirit has entered into the serpent that lives forever. In his priestess we see Hygeia, goddess of health and daughter of Asklepios. She and only she sees him when she comes to feed him with milk and honey cakes. Through her we know that the divine serpent raises his head as high as a man's breast; his eyes flash fire. It is too great a mystery for the eyes of mortal men."

Even at Olympia, Alexis had not felt such awe and wonder. He never lost that feeling in the time that followed, beginnning with his climb to Apollo's shrine on the mountainside. The priest who went with him was named Laos. He was a man of middle age, older than Aristes, thought Alexis. Within his beard his mouth had a look of kindness and in his face Alexis seemed to see the face of Asklepios. His black hair was still thick and curled to his shoulders. In the long white robe worn by priests of Asklepios, his stride was vigorous. After the sacrifice, alone with Alexis as they returned to Epidauros, he questioned him.

"I know that you are an Olympic victor and are here for your brother, whose eye is blinded. How did it happen?"

"He was boxing at Olympia against Glaukon of Tiryns."

"How does he feel toward Glaukon?"

"He feels hatred, of course."

"He too could have blinded his opponent?"

"That is true."

"His looks have been spoiled?"

"No, he still has the face of a god. At least, I think so. Everyone says so."

"He is fortunate. If a boxer goes on long enough, he is sure to end with the face of a beast, the bones thickened from receiving blows, ears and nose broken, teeth gone. What else does your brother like to do?"

"Nothing else."

Laos walked on in silence until they reached the sanctuary. Then he said, "You offered a wreath for your brother. The beauty of a wreath does not last. When it withers, we regard it as a sign that the struggle is still going on. There is always another contest."

The words were puzzling and Alexis did not know how to answer.

"Ask for a bed in the abaton," Laos said. "I will talk to you each day, and if you have dreamed, you should tell me. I will never repeat anything that you say. Your beautiful stepmother also is under my care. You should talk freely together. Words are the physicians of the mind. And she should walk; it will do her good."

Gorgo, having little to do, passed the day in listening to stories about miraculous cures and reported them to Melissa and Alexis. To encourage him, she told about a woman of Athens who had come to Epidauros, blind in one eye. She did not really believe in the cures she heard about, but Asklepios came to her in a dream and cut open her blind eye and poured in ointment. Then her told her to offer a silver pig in his temple because of her stupidity. When she woke, she was cured. Also, a former slave came. He had once run away from his master and been branded on the forehead as punishment. When he was freed he came to Epidauros and slept in the abaton with a cloth bound around his head. In the morning the mark of shame on the man's forehead was gone. It was found transferred to the cloth. Gorgo repeated this story again and again in the days that followed. It seemed to give her great satisfaction.

· 2 ·

On their second day at Epidauros Alexis began to walk with Melissa, and both benefited. Sometimes they talked to other suppliants, but more often they kept to themselves, speaking of Asini and the family at home. This time they followed a long wooded gorge that led down from Epidauros to the seacoast. They talked freely, sharing what Laos had said to each of them.

"He called you my beautiful stepmother," Alexis said, smiling.

Melissa smiled too, but shook her head. "He does not mean beautiful as your own mother was beautiful. To Laos, beauty means goodness, and I am not even good. I think things that are not good."

"You are very good, and you are beautiful, especially when you smile."

She refused to believe this but said that the rest and change of air might have improved her looks. "Besides, they bring me potions to drink and food cooked with special herbs. They say that the serpent god knows all of the healing plants. And you, Alexis?"

"I slept in the abaton last night. It was strange with the curtains blowing around me. I thought that spirits were trying to come through, though I knew it was only the wind. I could hear the voice of a priest in the distance, talking to someone who was drinking the bitter herbs, I think. Then I fell asleep. Laos has reminded me that true dreams come through gates of horn and false ones through gates of ivory. I am to tell him my dreams. But last night I had none."

"I did not dream on the first night," said Melissa, "but last night I thought I saw—your father. He was on a ship with a beautiful woman. She was veiled, but I could see her golden hair. Then they disappeared, ship and all, and I woke feeling very cold. I have told Laos and he says it is a false dream that came because I am afraid of losing your father to the sea or—some other way."

That night Alexis had a dream and in the morning told it to Laos. "It was nothing to do with Dion," he said. "I thought I saw my grandfather. He was sitting at home where he used to sit with all the family gathered round while he played his lyre and sang about Troy and the great deeds done there by the Greeks in the old days. We never hear the old songs at home now that he is gone."

"Where is the lyre?" asked Laos. "Not broken or lost?"

"No, Dion has it. Our grandfather gave it to him before he died, and told him to learn the songs."

"Then your dream does have something to do with Dion after all?"

"Perhaps it does," Alexis said slowly. "But Dion has no taste for music."

"The taste for music may come to him now that he can no longer box. When the gods take away one thing, something else is given."

"At school Dion never really learned the words," Alexis said doubtfully.

"But you did? And you could teach your brother what you know? When you go home, begin to recite the words with him. Tune the lyre and put it beside him. One day he may pick it up. One does not need sight to play the lyre. Remember, Homer was blind."

"Dion will not be blind," Alexis protested. "The god will heal him, isn't that true? I can see that Melissa is already being healed. Won't Asklepios do the same for Dion?"

"It is true, but there is more than one kind of healing, just as there is more than one kind of sickness," Laos answered. "All evil is a sickness." His deep-set eyes searched Alexis's face. "Why did your grandfather not give his lyre to you?"

"He said that I could not take it to some far place where I will be going."

"Ah. He was near death and saw things hidden from you. Well, we will talk again tomorrow."

Each day Laos seemed more wise and kind, as if he himself were Asklepios. Each day Alexis walked and talked with Melissa. Slowly, shyly, her words came at first, then more freely, always about Aristes—how he had looked when he asked for her hand in marriage, how he had taken command of the ship when he brought her from Crete to Asini, what designs he preferred in her weaving, how many days it had been since her last sight of him. She dreamed of him every night.

Sometimes Alexis laughed and shook his head, wondering. "I believe you think he is a god."

To which she answered simply, "I know he is a man."

As for Alexis's part, he told Melissa that he had few dreams, and none with any meaning. Then came a night toward the end of their second week at Epidauros when Alexis dreamed about Niki. He saw her as she had been when they were small children, sitting together on the beach at Asini while he built a sand palace like their father's palace on the cliff above them. He was finishing the

71

last wall and patting it smooth when suddenly she thrust her little feet forward, kicking his castle to pieces. Then she jumped up and ran away laughing, and he saw that she was no longer a child. Someone was following her, overtaking her, not he, but Glaukon, who looked at her as he had looked from his chariot on the road to Olympia. Glaukon caught her hand and held her, and suddenly a great wave came curling and arching over them and swept them away, and they were gone. When Alexis told this dream to Laos, they were walking on the mountain path that led to the shrine of Apollo. Laos stopped to look down on the sanctuary below them, and Alexis, pausing beside him, found his thoughts pouring out in a torrent of words.

"She will destroy us all. It is not only that she loves the man who injured her brother. Before that, Glaukon's father injured our father. He sailed away and left him to be robbed by pirates. It was years ago, but the gods have not forgotten and our family has never prospered since that time. One day soon I will kill Glaukon and settle the score." He drew a great breath and exhaled it with relief that the words were out, knowing that this relief was nothing compared to what he would feel when words became deeds.

Laos stood motionless. Then he said slowly, "I know what Neleus did. I was born in Tiryns."

Alexis drew back as if the priest had struck him.

"A moment ago I was your friend," said Laos. "Am I now your enemy because I was born in Tiryns?"

It seemed to Alexis that the earth trembled under his feet. Was it Apollo who had struck him, or struck the earth at his feet with a keen arrow shot from the almighty bow? He looked up at the sun now blazing high overhead and the unbearable brightness turned to a darkness in his eyes.

From his earliest days Alexis had believed that nothing good could come from Tiryns. Yet it was the home of this Laos, this priest, who seemed almost like a god, all wise and all kind. Tiryns and everyone living there should be crushed to earth, and he had sworn to strike the first blow. Yet to this man from Tiryns he had opened his mind freely and gratefully, trusting him to act as the agent through which Dion might be healed. And now he had revealed to Laos the thought that he had kept hidden from every other human being.

"Do not try to look into the face of Apollo. His radiance is too great for our eyes." It was Laos's voice and as Alexis looked once more into the face of the priest, he still saw the image of the sun. "It can happen," said Laos, "that a moment comes when the god and a soul meet. This may be the moment for you, Alexis. You have been nursing evil in your soul and one day it will be full grown. I have told you that all evil is a sickness. The man who damages another damages himself. You need to be healed as much as your brother needs it."

Alexis stood silent, trying to find words for his thoughts.

"I will leave you now," Laos said. "We will not talk again today. But your anger is no more than the stamp of a child's foot in the sand, compared with the anger of the gods. Leave revenge to them, if there must be revenge."

"But I do pray for revenge when I pray for my brother," Alexis objected.

"As for your prayers, remember how Homer says they are like poor old women, lame, wrinkled, and half blind, following in the footsteps of Sin, who rushes ahead, seeking to destroy all mankind. Still the prayers come hobbling along, and healing, because they are daughters of the great

73

god Zeus. If we have pity on them, they bless us and listen to our own prayers. If not, they ask Zeus to let us fall into sin, and so we are paid for our hardness of heart." Laos turned away and went down the path toward Epidauros.

Long after he had gone, Alexis stayed on the mountain thinking about what had been said between them. From where he stood he looked out over the hills that surrounded Epidauros and down on the sanctuary. Among its groves columns of smoke rose from the altar fires. To the east he could trace the path that led to the sea and above him arched the great blue dome of the sky. Earth, air, fire, water—the gods lived in all of them, and all were full of the glory of the gods. In harmony with this glory he had meant to become a path for the healing of Dion. Did he himself need to be healed? Could Laos have told the truth about that? All of his life he had known clearly and simply that he should love his home and family and hate his enemies. Now Laos was saying that hatred was a kind of sickness. To think about this further, he lay down at last on the carpet of heather that covered the mountain-side. In his mind there was no harmony, only turmoil. Presently he closed his eyes and slept.

When he woke, Peteos was standing beside him. "Laos said that I would find you here," he told Alexis. "Your stepmother is to drink the bitter herbs tonight and you can drink them too, if you like. Tomorrow you can return to Asini and bring back your guard to take your step-mother home. Laos asked me to tell you."

Looking up into the friendly face, Alexis felt strangely at peace. "I am ready," he said, and followed the young priest down the mountainside to Epidauros, pleased and somehow reassured by his cheerful face and the alert but relaxed way he moved.

"You are in training to do what Laos does?" Alexis asked.

"No, I will never be a philosopher like Laos, but they think I may have healing hands. It is a gift that Asklepios sometimes gives. Time will tell. I am being trained as a physician, learning how to use herbs and mix ointments and to clean and bind up wounds. Already I can make a salve and a potion from the juice of poppies to ease pain. Some day I will be able to treat fevers and prescribe diets. Both kinds of healing are necessary, you see. Prayer and sacrifice and purification and the interpretation of dreams, all of that is the work of the philosophers here at Epidauros. But we physicians have a saying: Prayer is very good, but one who calls on the gods must also do his part. You do not need my help, but I might help your brother. There is a salve for diseased eyes. I will give you some to take to him tomorrow."

Melissa had saved the best gifts for the last: a soft coverlet of her own weaving, sea blue, worked with a border of white ships, and a fine little statue made of terra cotta. It was the figure of a goddess holding a serpent in each hand. "It came from Crete," said Melissa. "I will offer her to the god. You give the coverlet, Alexis, because some day, no doubt, you will be a seafarer like your father."

Laos was at the altar of Asklepios when they came that night to pray and to make their offerings. "Toward morning the soul is free," he told them. "I will bring the bitter herbs to you then." Afterward they parted and went to their beds in the abaton.

Alexis lay awake listening to the wind blowing in the tops of the pine trees; so the waves sounded along the beach at home on a night of calm weather. Tomorrow he would be at Asini. He was not a distance runner, but if he paced himself right, he should be there by noon. In his mind he saw the road now, coming down from the highland farms, and he saw himself retracing that route until he came in sight of his father's barns and flocks and vineyards. Now half asleep, he saw someone like his father, yet not his father, handling the plough behind his oxen and driving a straight furrow as his father did. The man leaned down to test a clod of earth between his fingers and, seeming well satisfied, went on to the end of his field.

Alexis saw the beautiful farm more and more clearly and words began to fill his mind. Homer had sung the words to describe the wonderful designs on the shield of Achilles, and Telamon had made Alexis learn them by heart. "And the field grew black behind and looked as if it were being ploughed, though it was made of gold, for this was the great marvel of the shield. . ." In another part, workers were reaping with sharp sickles while behind them boys gathered up the grain and carried it to the binders, and among them the king was standing at the swathe, "rejoicing in his heart." On yet another part of the shield was a vineyard, teeming with clustered grapes. "Black were the grapes," said Homer, "and the golden vines hung on silver poles." Yet it was no finer than the vineyard at home, thought Alexis. Tomorrow he would see it all once again. Then mist and darkness covered the scene and Alexis knew no more until he saw through his closed eyelids a faint light. It was Laos parting the curtains beside the bed. He carried a small oil lamp and held out a cup. "If you are ready, it is the time," he said.

Alexis took the cup, but said, "I have dreamed already."

"You will dream again," said Laos.

The drink was bitter, but Alexis drank it down.

76

"The god will come to you," Laos told him, and went away.

For a long while Alexis lay waiting for the god to come, but the night was like any other night. At last he felt sleep pouring over him and let himself sink into it. Then in the darkness he saw a fiery light, round and brightly shining, radiant as the sun. Yet he could look straight into the full blaze and he saw that it was not the sun but the shield of Achilles with its handle toward him. He ran toward it and grasped it and ran on, his ears filled with the sound of a whirlwind and of shouting. But he was not afraid, because someone was running beside him and he knew that it was Asklepios, gleaming in golden armor. Then Alexis saw below him a blue bay circled with mountains, and the bay was filled with many ships. The voice of the god said to him clearly, "Have courage," and as he ran Alexis longed to look into the divine face. But suddenly darkness closed around him again and he saw no more. When he woke it was broad daylight and Laos was parting the curtains beside his bed.

"I have seen the god," said Alexis, and told Laos his two dreams of the shield of Achilles.

The priest stood motionless, listening, and still stood as if considering when Alexis had finished. At last he said, "You have dreamed true, once for your brother and once for yourself. Both dreams came to you through the gates of horn. Remember that the gods offered Achilles the choice of a long life or a brief glory, and both are good, but each man has his own destiny. The man with his hand on the plough and the king with his harvest are one and the same man, your brother, whose healing has begun. As for your second dream, you saw a bay. Was it the bay of Asini?"

"No, it was a place that I have never seen."

"Were the ships Greek ships?"

"I can't remember . . . no, I think their sails were not like our sails."

Laos seemed to withdraw into himself. Then he spoke again, as if reluctantly. "I cannot see all things clearly, but it comes to me that your grandfather was a prophet. Your foot is already on the road that he saw before you. The thing that you expect will not happen, but the god will show you the way. At the end of your road the shield of Achilles will be in your hand and you will be that shield. In the time of danger the god will be with you, putting courage into your heart, and all will be well with you."

"And Melissa?"

Laos smiled. "I have seen her this morning. She too dreamed of the god. She saw him coming up the path from the sea and he spoke to her in loving words. Of course it is a true dream. Who would not love such a woman? Now you should break your long fast. Ask Peteos for bread and milk."

Intending to find Peteos, Alexis dressed and stepped out into the sunshine. Then in the distance, to the east of the sanctuary, he saw Melissa. She was looking at a man who came toward her on the path that led up from the sea. Now they were together, their hands clasping, lips touching. Even far off there was no mistaking Aristes's broad shoulders, his look of command. Tied to his traveler's staff was a sack, which he was opening. He took something from it and put it around Melissa's neck. When they finally moved toward Alexis, he knew that neither had yet seen him. Aristes's head was bent toward Melissa's and they had no eyes except for each other.

They saw him at last and greeted him like travelers

just arrived from some strange and lovely faraway land.

"He has come," Melissa said joyfully, as if Alexis would not believe it without being told. Her eyes were bright, her cheeks flushed with rosy color. "I knew he would come. Last night in my dream I saw the god on the path from the sea, and this morning when I went to look . . . it was a miracle. And see, Alexis, your father has brought me a present from Crete."

It was a gold chain and a pendant shaped like two golden bees clinging to a circle of honeycomb.

"I found it in a goldsmith's shop," said Aristes. "It seemed meant for you and I thought, I don't know why, that I should come straight here to take you home. My ship is at the port below and the voyage will be easier than the road. Have you had enough of this place and will they let you go, both of you?"

"We are ready," Alexis told him. "This very day I was to return to Asini and bring back the guard. With your permission, Father, I will still go by the road. I have not had a good run for two weeks. I will tell them at home that you are coming." He looked from Aristes's face to Melissa's, remembering what she had told him about her first voyage to Asini as a bride. On this second voyage together they would not need him.

By noontime Alexis was on the road through the mountains and by late afternoon, sometimes running, sometimes walking, and already tired, he reached the ridge from which he would catch his first glimpse of the home farms. It was from there that he saw the smoke, not the thin thread from some peaceful hearth, but an ugly smear across the skyline where his father's barn stood.

When disaster strikes, what happened before is forgotten. Alexis did not know how he reached the barn. He only knew that he must have run farther and faster than he had ever run in his life. He found the barn in blackened ruins. Dion was there directing his father's farm laborers and working like a slave himself. With sacks and blankets they were beating out the destroying flames that still burst from the charred remnants of the walls, threatening to spread to other barns nearby.

A man came up to Alexis and he saw that it was Telamon, his face streaked with soot, his eyes red and wild. "Too late," he said. "The grain burned like a furnace. Your father's harvest is gone."

"How did it start?" Alexis asked miserably. Having nothing else to use, he tore off his tunic and began to beat the fire as if he could punish it for its crime against his father's harvest.

"Who knows how it started?" answered Telamon, working beside him. "We saw it about noon, but it may have been smoldering for hours. I can tell you this. Some men from Tiryns were seen hunting in these hills last night."

·IV·

To Tiryns

·1·

W ITH the burning of the barn, Alexis's long-smolder-
ing wish for revenge against Tiryns burst into a
flame that seemed to rage upward from the soles
of his feet until it filled his brain and drove out all other
thoughts. He knew that he could not bring down the might
of that walled city single-handed; that must be done some
day by all the citizens of Asini and all the allies they could
muster. He could not even confront Neleus alone; Aristes
must do that, because as kings they were equals. But Aristes
had delayed for reasons unknown to Alexis. Dion as older
son was not the man he had been before Olympia; his
fighting days were over, unless the salve from Epidauros
healed his eyes. That might, or might not, happen. It remained for Alexis to be the avenger. He could not control
his rage much longer and he poured it out to Telamon
and Dion.

"When a man feels that rage, he has the strength of a
god," said Telamon. "Your father will feel the same. You
will see him take action now." Dion agreed.

But the next day when Aristes brought Melissa home
from Epidauros, he did not take action. After riding up
alone to the hill farm to survey the ruins of the year's
harvest, he returned to the palace with the look of a

broken man and shut himself into the room that he shared with Melissa. Alexis, waiting with Dion in the courtyard, could hear their voices raised in grief, then lowered in prolonged conversation.

At last the door opened and Aristes came out. He looked agitated but it was clear that he had made up his mind.

Dion stepped forward to meet his father with something of his old spirit in his face. "What have you decided, Father? Do we go to Tiryns and challenge them?"

"No," said Aristes. "We will not go, neither I nor you. Your mother says that we have no evidence, and she is right."

Alexis cried out, "No evidence! We don't need evidence! Who else—"

"Perhaps a traveler taking shelter in the barn for the night. Perhaps bandits. Melissa says that many have been seen lately."

Melissa says. Alexis groaned inwardly. This was what came of consulting a woman, even the best of them. In the past, Aristes would have consulted Abas and got an answer based on the honor of Asini and of the family. Melissa's answer was based on her love for Aristes and her fear of losing him.

"Melissa has earned the right to speak on this matter," Aristes went on. "It is she who manages everything when I am away, and she has done it so well that we can live without hardship until the next harvest. I am paying my debts, little by little. My creditors are not unreasonable." He gave a wry smile. "They do not threaten to sell me into slavery for my debts. The grape harvest has been good this year and the olives look promising. We have much to be thankful for. Melissa asks me not to risk losing all we have in an attack on Neleus, and I have agreed. You must abide by that agreement."

When old Chrysis heard of this, she nodded. "Melissa's advice is good," she said to Alexis. "Remember how your grandfather used to say, 'Do nothing too much'? They say those words are written over the shrine of Apollo at Delphi. Do not frown, Alexis. Remember how Abas would sing from Homer, 'Young men are quick to move this way and that, but an older man thinks before he acts.' "

Alexis knew that verse, but it did not appeal to him. What Niki said was worse. "Don't you see? Father has fallen in love with Melissa. Now they both want to live to have another child." Alexis worried too about Niki herself. She was thin and pale, full of moods. It seemed to him that she was learning her household duties willingly, but sometimes he heard her singing a sad little love song: "At midnight when all were sleeping, Love came to my door and knocked. 'Who is there?' I asked. And Love said, 'Open. I am only a little boy, standing in the rain, lost in the moonless night.' Then I lit my lamp and opened the door to him, a little boy with wings and a bow and quiver. I sat him by the hearth until his hands were warm and he said, 'Come let us see whether the string of my bow is damaged by the rain.' He draws the bow and lets fly an arrow, wounding my heart. And he laughs at me. 'My bow is not damaged, but your heart will ache.' "

Once Alexis even heard her singing under her breath the refrain of a song no nice girl should sing. It was about a lovesick girl, holding her lover by spells and charms. Niki must have learned that song at Olympia, thought Alexis, when she had got away from Gorgo and was wandering about alone among the crowds, or with Glaukon. Much harm had been done at Olympia, harm to Niki as well as to

Dion. Love! That kind of love caused nothing but trouble.

The autumn passed and Alexis himself took no action against the enemies at Tiryns. At the beginning of winter two events occurred that changed everything. Telamon left Asini, a free man, and Aristes arranged for Alexis to be trained in wrestling and throwing the javelin at the gymnasium.

On a cold gray morning of early winter Telamon paid the last coins that would release him from slavery. As he put them into Aristes's hand he said, "Now I breathe as a free man again. I suppose this is the last time I will ever see you, so now I will tell you that you treated me well. At least I was not beaten or branded."

Aristes shrugged. "If you had tried to run away, it might have been different." He held out the coins. "You were a good teacher to my sons. Keep these. You may need them."

But Telamon refused with a smile. "I feel my pride coming back," he said.

Melissa gave him a warm cloak, a close-fitting cap, and a pair of leather boots lined with felt. He wept and accepted them, clinging to her hand. "When the north wind blows, and when I am far away at night in a freezing rain, I will think of you and thank you."

To Chrysis he bowed respectfully, only wishing her long life, but by the time he came to say goodbye to the younger members of the family, he was in high spirits. They went with him as far as the landward gate of the town.

"Where are you going?" Dion asked.

"I will find a ship bound for Samos. If my old father still lives, I will beg his forgiveness for running away from home."

"And then?"

"To Athens, of course, and a real school. If I have been able to knock something into wooden heads at Asini, it will be paradise to teach bright Athenian boys. By the way, Dion, you showed some slight promise with the lyre. Your grandfather's lyre has been silent too long. I have put it in tune for you. Try your hand at it again." He gave Dion a playful blow to the chest and turned to Alexis more soberly. "If you, Alexis, ever have a chance to go to Athens, find a philosopher and sit at his feet. It would not be wasted on you."

Alexis was pleased by this faint praise, but shook his head. "Impossible. You know my father cannot afford luxuries now." He looked closely at Telamon and asked, "Are you growing a beard?"

Telamon passed a hand over his jaws and spoke with satisfaction. "You have noticed already? I never wanted a beard when I was free, but when I was a slave and was forbidden to grow one, I found I wanted one more than anything. Look for me if you ever come to Athens. I will have the longest and thickest beard in the city." With a backward wave, he strode off.

From this time Alexis went with Dion every afternoon to the ground outside the gymnasium where other boys of his age were being trained in throwing the javelin and in wrestling, two sports that would stand him in good stead when the time came for his military service. As winter came on, Aristes remarked that Alexis's shoulders were already broader and stronger. He gave him Abas's sword and spear. Alexis hung them on the wall above his bed and kept them sharp and shining. Because of his new strength, he did well in throwing the javelin and found that he could hold his own with the best of the wrestlers. The wrestling always attracted a crowd around the sandy square where the athletes met, and the cheering and joking of the spectators added to the excitement of the lesson. Alexis liked to imagine that every opponent was Glaukon; he relished the coming to grips, the hot struggle that followed until a lucky thrust of a foot sent both wrestlers into the sand or a catch under the thigh tore one contestant off the ground, instantly to be hurled down again, stunned and breathless. Two throws out of three made a victory.

After a lesson came a friendly bout with Dion. The salve from Epidauros had not helped Dion, but failing eyesight was no great disadvantage in wrestling. Later in the bathhouse they shared the pleasure of scraping off sand and sweat, rinsing in fresh water, and rubbing down with sweet oil.

Dion looked more cheerful these days. As his sight grew dim, his other senses seemed to grow keener. He spoke about the good smell of wood smoke and of freshly baked bread. He was learning to judge by feeling the quality of earth and of sheep's wool. The taste of fish, of cheese, fruit, and wine brought some comment from him at every meal. He sought out friendships as he had never done before. Alexis remembered the words of the priest at Epidauros: "When the gods take away one thing, something else is given." And, "There is more than one kind of healing." Dion was no longer a boxer; but he was becoming a whole man.

When the olive harvest began, he went with his father to help direct the beating down of the fruit from the trees. He made a short voyage with Aristes to sell wine, and on the return, worked with the sailors in beaching the ship for the winter. One night as the family sat around the fire in the courtyard, he brought out his grandfather's lyre and

88

struck a few notes; the family exchanged glances, hoping for more. Dion soon put the instrument back in its corner, but it was a start, thought Alexis; it was at least a start.

"Sing 'May the gods grant you your heart's desire,' " said Aristes, and when Dion said he would need practice to sing properly from Homer's lines, his father sang the verses without accompaniment, looking at Melissa: " 'May the gods grant you your heart's desire, a husband and a happy home. For there is nothing finer than when a man and woman live together in harmony, confounding their enemies and delighting their friends, as they themselves know better than anyone.' "

Niki, seated on a stool at Alexis's side, whispered, "See how she looks at him. She is going to have another child, I am sure of it." Suddenly she turned her face away and ran from the courtyard up the staircase to the women's quarters, closing the door behind her.

If Melissa and Aristes were happy, thought Alexis, let them be happy, but Niki's lovesick behavior filled him with anger. He was even more angry when Gorgo took him aside the following day and said, "Talk to your sister. The watchman on the tower has seen her on the beach with a man."

"Who was the man?"

"I do not know. He came by boat, a small boat with a sail. They were far down the beach, but the watchman says the man was young and tall, fair-haired. He stood close to Niki, talking. Then he left, sailing around the point as if going to Nauplion—or Tiryns."

"It was Glaukon, of course. Why did the watchman not send word to my father?"

"He felt sorry for Niki. He said that if she was to have

a beating, it would be his fault, yet he could not be silent. He left it to me to tell someone in the family, if it had to be told. Besides, he says his work is to watch out for pirates and armed vessels, not for little unarmed boats."

"What a fool! And now you leave it to me."

"Because you are closest to Niki. You should warn her not to see this man. If she will not listen, you must tell her father."

The slaves always knew what was happening before the master knew, Alexis thought bitterly. He lay sleepless through the night, convinced that the man on the beach was Glaukon and that he would come again. As Paris, prince of Troy, had stolen Helen of Sparta away from her home, and caused the Trojan War, so Glaukon meant to steal Niki. If that happened, war between Asini and Tiryns would follow, with Asini unprepared and with no allies committed to the fight. Or suppose that his father beat Niki and locked her up. He could not keep her a prisoner forever, and he would not force her to marry some other man against her will. It was of no use to talk to Niki. His dream at Epidauros had been true; she had kicked down his sand castle and now the sea was about to sweep her away in the arms of Glaukon. Aphrodite, goddess of love, came from the sea, and she and her son Eros, the boy with the bow and arrows, were too powerful for Niki to resist. As long as Glaukon lived, she would love him; therefore Glaukon must die. Last spring he had come to Asini and Alexis had said, "If you come again, I will kill you." Well, Glaukon had come again. Alexis felt in his soul the hatred that was sweeter than honey and he knew that he was ready.

While it was still dark, he left his bed and put on a sheepskin coat over his tunic. He tied on his hunting shoes and took from the wall his grandfather's spear and the sword in its belted sheath. The handle of the sword fitted his grasp as if it had been made for him. Dion turned on his side but did not waken.

The guard opened the outer door at Alexis's whispered order, and he passed through, asking any gods who might be listening to bless his family and his home. When the landward gate of the town had opened and closed again behind him, he prayed for all of Asini and set out on the road that led north to Nauplion and Tiryns. From the solitary hut of a hill farm a thread of smoke was rising. Some poor farmer must be feeding the embers of last night's fire, lighting his small lamp and preparing to grind a little of his miserable store of wheat. Alexis asked a blessing on all the poor men whose fate, for good or ill, depended on Asini, and walked on swiftly toward Tiryns, pacing himself so that he would be fresh for what he was about to do. His plan was to find Glaukon and offer to fight him in single combat; Glaukon could not, in honor, refuse. If he killed Glaukon, that would end matters. If Glaukon was the victor, Niki would never marry the man who had killed her brother, and Alexis intended to fight to the death.

At a high point on the road beyond Nauplion he stopped, the north wind blowing against him from an ugly sky. Before him the vast walls and towers of Tiryns crowned their clouded hilltop. To the west, a stone causeway led across marshy ground to the sea, a mile away. To the east was the ramp where he would find access to the citadel, if he was to be allowed to enter. As Alexis surveyed the awesome sight, there came into his mind the image of Diomedes, youngest of the Greek heroes at Troy, Diomedes of the loud war cry. This was his country and his blood still flowed in the veins of men sprung from the same soil. In spite of his youth it was Diomedes who always took on the dangerous task at Troy. Athene had put such valor into his heart that the Trojans feared him most of all. "He fights with fury and fills men's souls with panic," they said. "His rage is beyond all bounds. He is the bravest of the brave." Alexis moved forward.

Below him were olive groves whose thick gnarled trunks and twisted branches would provide some cover. He left the road and took to the shelter of the trees until he found a heap of leaves where he hid his sword and spear. Unarmed, he walked on quickly to the foot of the great fortress and followed a rough path to its eastern side. Now there loomed above him wall after wall, tower after tower, built by giants, each stone higher than a man's head. Here he must find the way in.

Now the ramp lay just ahead, narrow, long, and steep. He began to climb it, keeping close to the wall. Beyond a doubt he was being watched from above and would meet guards at a gateway when he reached the top. Would they kill him outright? No; Glaukon had come alone to Asini, and survived. He turned through an opening in the thick stone wall and saw two guards directly ahead of him. Helmeted and fully armed, they barred his way.

"I am Alexis, son of Aristes, king of Asini," he shouted. "I demand to speak to Glaukon, prince of Tiryns."

No sooner had the words left his mouth than the guards seized him by the arms and led him through the gateway, more a prisoner than a guest. He was hurried unceremoniously through a series of turns, gateways, and colonnades, stopping at last in a large open courtyard. Alexis was awed. The walls were painted in the ancient style with pictures of brave heroes and beautiful women in scenes of hunting, of soldiery, and of worship. The floor too was painted and decorated with patterns of dolphins and octopuses. Against one wall stood a carved stone seat, fit for royalty, and Alexis judged this to be the throne room of Neleus. Here he was left with one of the guards while the other disappeared into an inner chamber. Had the palace at Asini ever looked like this? wondered Alexis. If so, neglect and old wars had done their worst. He felt humbled by the splendor of Tiryns, and he felt anger rising.

The guard soon came from the inner room and signaled that Alexis was to enter it. He walked through a narrow doorway into a pleasant chamber, lighted from above by an opening in the ceiling. Through the opening, smoke rose from a fire of sweetly scented wood that burned in the center of the floor. By the fire a woman was seated at a loom with a servant behind her. The shuttle was filled with a fine purple wool.

The guard said, "Lady, this is the boy we saw coming."

She stopped her work and looked up at Alexis, saying, "Yes, you are still a boy. If you are really Alexis, son of Aristes, go home to Asini. Go in peace, but never return."

He thought he had never seen a woman so beautiful. Her dark curling hair was held in place by a blue band and pinned up at the back of her head to show the graceful neck. Blue eyes beneath strongly marked brows, the turn of the delicate cheeks, the finely proportioned nose, all told him who she was, even before she said, "I am Glaukon's mother."

"I came to find him," Alexis told her.

"Neither he nor my husband are here," she said. "You want to prevent my son from marrying your sister, but you cannot do that. If he has won her heart, he will have her, in spite of you. If she does not want him, you have nothing to fear. I have no more to say to you."

This calm and queenly woman did not look or sound angry, only sad. Alexis felt that she had not meant to insult him. But even as he tried to answer in a way befitting a prince of Asini, the two guards again seized him and hurried him from the room, through a court behind the palace, and on to a tower in the west wall. There they thrust him out and bolted a heavy door behind him. A long stone staircase led down to a postern gate far below. So, he thought, he had come into Tiryns through the front entrance, and the guards had thrown him out at the back. Humiliated and shamefaced, he stood fuming at the top of the staircase. Boy. They had called him a boy.

Even when events seem to happen by chance, there is a design in them, though only the gods may know the meaning of the design. Looking down from the tower, Alexis saw in the distance, beyond leafless orchards, vineyards, and bare ploughed fields, the near end of the stone causeway. A man was walking rapidly along the causeway toward the sea, armed with a sword and a spear. There was no mistaking him. It was Glaukon.

Alexis ran down the staircase. The guard at the gate in the wall let him go through without a question and he did not again slacken speed until he found his weapons under the leaves in the olive grove. Then he ran for the causeway. Once on it, he found its smooth hard-packed surface as fine a race course as he could wish for.

Glaukon was now on the slope that led down to the water. A mist was stretched out across the marshy land,

and thickets of reed hid the shore. So much the better. Alexis would overtake Glaukon on the beach, unseen by any guards who might be watching from the west tower. He saw no guard on the beach, and thanked the gods. Now he too was on the slope and still Glaukon was unaware of him. He had left the causeway and was walking along the excellent harbor of Tiryns where the fleet of Neleus lay, small boats, broad-beamed trading vessels, and long slender black warships with curved prows, careened on the sand. Except for Glaukon, there was no sign of life. The wind had died; the sea was flat and empty. Only one small boat was tied up at a slip as if ready to sail. So this was why Glaukon had come to the shore alone at such a time. He intended to make for Asini today, to meet Niki and steal her away.

Alexis leaped from the causeway and shouted, "Dog with the heart of a chicken, turn and fight!" He drew his sword from its sheath and ran along the shore. Glaukon stopped, turned, and stood still, amazement written in his face.

"Do not be a fool," he said evenly. "I do not want to fight you."

"You have no choice," Alexis retorted. "Either I will kill you or be killed."

"You speak like a child," said Glaukon, "but I will answer you as a reasonable man. Did you come because of your sister? Let me tell you that she is mine by her own choice. When the time comes I will take her, but today is not the day."

At these words, rage welled up in Alexis as if he saw through a bloody mist. "You lie!" he shouted. He ran forward, raised his spear, and aimed it at Glaukon's heart. Glaukon dropped his own spear and leaped aside, seizing

Alexis's sword arm and flinging him to his knees. The thrust of the spear sent it quivering into the sand. The sword fell out of reach. Glaukon flung his own sword after it.

"I will not fight you with weapons," he said.

Kneeling in the sand, Alexis threw his weight against Glaukon's thigh with a wrestler's hold, knocked him sprawling on his back, then pinned him down. But not for long. With a convulsion of muscle, Glaukon freed one arm and struck a blow that jerked Alexis's head back and blurred his vision. Then he recovered and lunged for Glaukon's throat.

While they fought like animals locked in a death struggle on the sand, two men came silently from among the reeds that edged the shore. Suddenly Alexis felt hands gripping his own throat from behind, choking off his breath, pulling him away. Had there been guards from Tiryns on the beach after all? He caught one glimpse of a man astride of Glaukon with a heavy stick in his hand. Not guards from Tiryns. Pirates. He saw the stick descending once, twice, on Glaukon's head. Then darkness closed in.

·V·

To Athens

·1·

THE PIRATES, who had landed at Tiryns before dawn, had tied up the small boat at a slip and wounded the guard by a mischance when he resisted capture. The marauders had then gone to forage at the low-lying farms. They had got no booty except for a pile of oxhides and were about to take off when the fight between Alexis and Glaukon began on the beach. Now they had two fine specimens for the slave market, as well as the lowly guard, who already lay trussed up in the boat.

Tying up Alexis and Glaukon with the ease of experts, they threw them into the boat on top of the oxhides and rowed back to the waiting vessel. The captain would be pleased when they returned to the ship, which was anchored offshore, covered by mist and hidden by a point of land. It had a crew of vagabonds from all parts of the Mediterranean, the captain being Phoenician, an experienced sailor of a hardy breed who carried out their raids at every season of the year. He spoke a little of several tongues, in his own way, having stolen, kidnapped, and sold his cargoes on many islands of the Aegean sea and many ports of the Greek mainland.

At sight of the three captives his men had brought from Tiryns, he said, "Excellent. Put them in the hold. Do nothing that would leave a mark on them. They will bring a good price."

When Alexis opened his eyes, he did not know how much time had passed. He was lying on his back in the hold of the ship, bound hand and foot. Above, on each side, was a tier of five benches and foot rests. By the light from a hatch in the deck, he saw that he was lying among jars and sacks under one of these tiers. Oars lay fore and aft along the benches. The ship must be under sail in the open sea, where rowers were not needed. He heard the sound of men's feet on the deck and the slap of waves against the hull. He smelled hemp and pitch, salt fish, and oil. Then he twisted to his side and saw Glaukon. He too was bound and lay pale and still, but he was breathing. Beyond Glaukon lay the motionless body of another man.

Alexis groaned and wept to think what a fool he had been. That little boat had not been waiting for Glaukon, but for pirates, who would sell both of them into slavery. He had never thought it could happen to him, a king's son and an Olympic victor, but only to others who were not of noble birth or who were less strong and intelligent. Now, through his own folly, he, a free-born Greek, was a captive and would soon be a slave, if he guessed the pirates' intentions correctly. He who had been safe at home with his well-loved family had lost everything, including his grandfather's spear and the treasured sword with the letter Alpha marked on its handle—Alpha for Abas. No doubt the pirates had them. What had possessed him to think that he, single-handed, could bring Tiryns to its knees? "Do nothing to excess," said the shrine of Apollo at Delphi. And at Epidauros, Laos, that good, wise priest, had told him, "The man who damages another, damages himself." Alexis groaned again.

At the sound, Glaukon opened his eyes. He turned his head to look at the third man and Alexis heard him say, "Dead. Ambushed." So, thought Alexis, this was why there had been no guard on the beach. The man had already been tied up and thrown into the little boat after a fatal blow.

For a long while Glaukon tossed and twisted as if delirious, sighing and moaning. Alexis heard, "Niki . . . lost . . . no escape . . ."

No escape. But why not escape? Somehow he would work loose from the ropes that bound him. Then he would leap into the sea and trust to the gods. His own father had done the same, and, like Odysseus, had lived to tell the tale. Alexis prayed to Poseidon that he might somehow get free of his bonds. Almost at once, as if in answer to that prayer, a man appeared in the hatchway above and let himself down into the hold. From his air of command Alexis correctly guessed him to be the captain of the ship. He was small and wiry, with a dark skin and a pointed beard. At his waist he carried a dagger with which he quickly cut the ropes that bound his prisoners. He examined Glaukon's head with a grunt of dissatisfaction, bent over the guard, feeling for a heartbeat, and gave an angry shout.

Two sailors in dark ragged tunics leaped into the hold and hoisted the guard's dead body to the deck. There was the sound of a splash. Then the two sailors again jumped down into the hold and cowered, trembling, while the captain seized them by the hair and knocked their heads together. After a long harangue he sent them scurrying up to the deck again with kicks and curses to speed them on their way. Now he turned his attention to Alexis and Glaukon. He ran his hands over their arms and shoulders, felt the muscles of their legs, speaking in a sort of Greek whose meaning was clear, if the accent and the words were not. The prisoners were to obey without question; otherwise it would be the worse for them.

When the captain had swung himself up through the hatch and disappeared, Alexis looked at Glaukon, who lay silent. His face was bruised. Dark streaks of blood had trickled from his scalp and matted the hair at his forehead. His body and tunic were caked with sand and dried sweat. Putting out his hand, Alexis felt an arm as cold as stone. If the pirates had saved him the trouble of killing Glaukon, the thought did not please him. He hated Glaukon, but he hated the pirates more. When all was said and done, he and Glaukon were Greeks; the pirates, barbarians. He had wanted revenge for the sake of justice, and this death would not be justice. Glaukon should have a chance to live and fight again against their common enemy. Alexis slipped off his sheepskin coat and laid it over Glaukon's body.

Soon afterward, a young sailor brought a pitcher of water. He washed Glaukon's wounds and poured into them a little of some liquid from a small vial. He was sponging the bloody and grimy face when Glaukon opened his eyes and said, "So I am not to die after all."

"If you die, my life will pay for it," the sailor answered grimly.

Alexis recognized a familiar accent. "You are from Samos?"

"How did you know?"

"I know by your speech. I had a teacher from Samos."

"The speech of Samos is the best in Greece. You were lucky. And now you are lucky again, because I can explain matters to you. My name is Milo. The captain has ordered me to keep both of you alive and in good condition until we reach Athens. You must do your part too. Here is warm water. Wash yourselves."

He returned with salt fish, a sack of olives and figs, and a jar of wine mixed with fresh water. He watched while they ate and drank. "Tomorrow you will exercise at the oars," he said to Alexis. "Your friend too, if he is fit for it. If you do not look fit at Athens, you will end in the silver mines and finally as meat for dogs. I tell you this in friendship because you are Greek."

"Where are we now?" Alexis asked.

"The first lesson a slave should learn is not to ask questions," said Milo shortly.

"I am no slave," Alexis burst out. "We are freeborn Greeks, and you are a filthy pirate. You are nothing."

"Be silent," muttered Glaukon. "Don't you know what they can do?"

"You are wise," Milo said to him. "Try to put some wisdom into the head of this one and save me the trouble."

When he had gone, Alexis lay looking up at the gray sky above the hatch. He must try to escape at all costs. If he died in the attempt, death would be better than slavery. As night fell, the hold became black except for the flickering light of a fire burning in a sandpit on deck. The wind died and sailors came down to man the oars, keeping a rhythm set by the shrill note of a flute played by a man at the hatch. At last the notes ceased and the rowers drew in their oars and went on deck again. Alexis heard the sound of an anchor being dropped. Then a piece of sailcloth was pulled over the hatch and tied down so that the hold was in total darkness. There was a sound of men moving over the side of the ship and of the small boat bumping against the hull.

103

Glaukon said under his breath, "They are going ashore for the night, but they will have left a guard."

"Still, this is the best chance to get away," Alexis said.

"Not for me. Not yet. Perhaps later, some other way, when I get back my strength. Listen. There are at least two guards up there."

Alexis judged that this was true. He heard talk, then laughter. "They will be eating and drinking," he said. "If they drink enough, they may sleep. I need something to cut my way out." He felt about him in the dark and touched the pitcher that Milo had left behind. "A shard will do," he said.

Presently the guards began to sing. Alexis broke the pitcher with a blow against the hull, but the guards paid no heed to the sound below. They continued to sing. Alexis lay still, biding his time until he thought the guards had drunk enough to muddle their wits. Testing the edges of broken pottery, he found one sharp enough to do his work. Then he climbed to a rowing bench at one corner of the hatch and reached out under the sailcloth. His fingers felt a rope where he had expected to find one and he set to work with his shard, using the noise made by the sailors to cover his own noise.

At last the talk and singing became senseless and stopped. "If I ever see you again, remember that we have not finished our fight," he said into the darkness. He pulled himself up into the hatch and crawled out from under the sailcloth onto the deck. Two guards lay in drunken sleep by the fire. Alexis slipped over the side of the ship and dropped into the sea.

It was bitter cold. Alexis clung to the ship, getting his bearings. The pirates had gone down into their boat on this side, therefore he guessed that this might be the direction toward land. Did he imagine or really hear the sound of waves breaking against rocks? He struck out toward that sound.

From the ship the water had seemed calm, but swimming in it he found himself now on the crest of a surge, now in the trough between high waves that looked ready to break over him and draw him down to the depths. Only the will to survive gave him the strength to swim on, and one memory put courage in his heart. His father Aristes had swum to shore when his ship had been sunk by pirates; and long, long before that, the great Odysseus had done the same.

Now, when Alexis needed the words most, they came to him again as he had recited them many times in school: "For two nights and two days he was tossed about in the swelling sea, expecting death. But when Dawn with her fair hair brought the third day, the wind fell, and as he was lifted on a great wave, he saw land near by and swam on. When he was within earshot of the shore, and heard the thunder of the sea against the reefs . . ." Alexis already heard that thunder, and long before dawn he should reach the coast. Odysseus had almost been crushed against a terrible crag, but he had prayed to Zeus and had come safely to shore at the mouth of a river. The pirates must have known of such a place, where they could beach their boat. Alexis prayed to Zeus that he too might find a safe landing place.

At that moment, a wave lifted him up and he caught a glimpse of a fire. There was a beach, then, among the rocks, nearer than he had dared to hope, but the pirates were there. He must swim along the shore, away from that beach, and pray that the waves would not dash him against the rocks but carry him along the shore to some spot where he could land unseen.

Beyond the beach to the left he saw the sharp crags against which waves roared and surged, but he was swept past them, still in deep water, then past a wall of smooth rock. Suddenly a wave cast him down. He felt the scrape and grind of pebbles and clawed his way to shore in a little cove. There he lay, vomiting salt water and gasping for breath. At last the cold black wind from the sea forced him, shivering, to his feet. He must find shelter somewhere or die of the cold. Above the cove, cliffs rose up, crowned with black trees. Up these cliffs he made his way on all fours, like an animal, his hands and legs torn by the rocks, and found himself in an olive grove.

The ancient branches were bare, their leaves in heaps on the ground. Alexis raised his arms in a brief salute of thanks to Zeus. Then he found a hollow under a tree and covered himself with a blanket of leaves. Odysseus too had climbed from the sea to the shelter of an olive grove. It was an omen, thought Alexis. The gods meant him to live.

He fell asleep smiling and dreamed that a beautiful princess came to his rescue as the princess Nausicaa had come to the rescue of Odysseus. She let him wash in the river and gave him fresh clothing and sweet oil for his skin, so long stung and crusted by the salt water. She led him to her father's fine city with walls and towers like those of Tiryns. And he was welcomed in through groves of trees and flowering meadows and gardens of pear trees and pomegranates and apple trees and straight on to the palace that gleamed like the sun and the moon. And the golden doors opened before him in welcome and all was light and shining. All about him the people of the palace were working or playing or eating and drinking. And in the inmost chamber he saw the queen sitting by the fire, weaving a web of purple wool as she sat against a pillar with her maidens behind her. At first he thought she was Glaukon's mother, and then he saw that she was Niki, and she was leaning toward him, offering him a cup of honey-sweet wine.

Then, callused hands closed around his neck and he woke, his eyes starting from their sockets. This was no dream. When the fingers relaxed their hold on his throat and his vision cleared, he saw the face of the pirate captain glaring down at him and spitting out words that were all too clear: "Slave . . . escape . . . punish . . ." Behind him stood Milo. He was carrying a jar and a sack, stolen no doubt from some farm in a pre-dawn raid, and he looked with dismay on the runaway they had stumbled upon in the olive grove.

The captain jerked Alexis to his feet, tied his hands behind him with a leather belt, and prodded him forward along the brow of the cliff. There was a steep path down to the beach where the pirates had camped for the night. Here Alexis fell, cutting his knees and bloodying his nose. The captain pulled him to his feet and held him upright, pushing him ahead. He saw the sailors around their fire, laughing and pointing at the procession coming down the path. They were obviously amazed that the captive had escaped and triumphant that he had been retaken. Alexis supposed they would not kill him, because he and Glaukon would bring more than all the rest of the ship's cargo; every man had a stake in their being delivered alive at the slave market. But his mouth was dry with fear. He knew what happened to runaway slaves.

They threw him into the boat, swarmed on board

themselves, and manned the oars. Then the ship loomed above him. They hauled him on deck, tossed him down on his back, and held him fast. At the captain's order, Milo brought Glaukon from the hold and bound him to the mast. "You there, watch and remember," he said.

From a little sack he took a silver coin welded to a metal handle. Holding it in a pair of tongs, he heated it at the fire in the sandpit. Alexis closed his eyes and clenched his teeth. No god would come to his rescue, and he could do nothing to save himself, but he could endure. He prayed that he would not disgrace himself, his family, and Asini. At Olympia he had called himself a free-born Greek. Free-born, free-born. Someone was holding his head so that he could not move it. Then in the center of his forehead he felt the pressure of the brand and a blinding pain that blotted out everything he had ever known until that moment. When the pressure of the brand stopped, the pain went on and on. Through the burning and throbbing Alexis heard the captain's voice and understood the words, "King Darius." He had been branded with the mark of a Persian coin then, and he would carry that mark as long as he lived.

Afterward they dropped him into the hold and threw Glaukon down after him. Neither of them had made a sound. They lay there in silence for a long while. Then Glaukon said in a low voice, "No Spartan could have done better." Alexis heard in amazement.

Glaukon had said the words. At the moment of his own extreme pain and shame, his enemy had been forced to do him justice. Truly, as the oracle at Olympia had told Niki, "The gods find a way that we did not expect." Was this the beginning of Alexis's revenge? If so, its taste was sweet.

· 2 ·

Soon afterward, Milo came with a pitcher and two cups. "Drink this, both of you," he said. "After what has happened, both should sleep." The drink was wine, with a bitter flavor, and Alexis knew that he had tasted something like it once before. When he had emptied the cup, he lay with closed eyes waiting for sleep to come. The bitter herbs at Epidauros. That was where he had tasted them, on the night of his dreaming. He felt something cool on his forehead and heard Milo's voice. "Lie still. I have put a poultice of mandrake leaves on the burn. There was mandrake root in the potion. It brings the sleep that eases pain."

True to his promise, sleep came, and with it the dreaming. Alexis seemed to be in bright sunlight at Epidauros on the mountain with the good priest Laos who had been born at Tiryns. Laos was saying, "Compared with the anger of the gods, your anger is no more than the stamp of a child's foot in the sand. Leave revenge to the gods." Someone—was it Peteos, the young priest, or Milo the pirate?—laid a cool cloth on Alexis's burning forehead, and the pain was gone. He heard the voice of Laos again. "In the time of danger, the god will put courage in your heart." Then clouds covered the sun and impregnable Tiryns loomed above Alexis, but he passed easily through the great stone walls and entered the inner chamber. A beautiful woman sat by the fire. "I am Glaukon's wife," she said. "Talk to him." And it was Niki.

Alexis woke, his heart pounding with anger. Were these true dreams that had come to him through the gates of horn, or only delusions coming through the gates of

109

ivory? The sky was black above the hatchway, but he saw Milo's face bending over him by the light of a small lamp. Milo dipped the poultice in cold water and laid it again on Alexis's forehead. He examined Glaukon's head and looked satisfied.

"You should have been a doctor," said Alexis.

"And instead, I am a filthy pirate. I am nothing, as you said. Sleep again." Milo filled the cups. This time the drink was mixed with honey, and there was no taste of bitter herbs.

"It seems you are healing me," said Glaukon. "Whoever you are, I am grateful. Where did you learn medicine?"

"In Samos, of course. We know everything in Samos. We learn from all the people of Asia and afterward we tell the other Greeks."

In the gray light of dawn Milo came once more, this time with wine and water to wash down a fistful of bread for each of the captives. "Eat now," he said. "Afterward you must row, and put your backs into it." He examined Glaukon's head and Alexis's burn. "The brave heal quickly. I advise you to look strong." He jerked his thumb upward toward the deck. "Otherwise he may tie you flat on your bench with your head sticking through the oar hole. It is a habit he learned in King Darius's navy."

"Then why do you stay with him?" Alexis asked, under his breath, "you who know medicine like the priests at Epidauros?"

"I am ashamed to stay," came the muttered answer, "but do you think I want to end like you with a brand on my forehead? No, I would not be so lucky as you. We have orders that you are to reach Athens with no mark of torture on you. What would my fate be if they caught me? We will talk again." Milo raised his voice. "From Tiryns I

110

cannot expect much, but at least you must know an oar when you see one."

"I am from Asini," Alexis said coldly.

Milo laughed. "From Asini? It has not been heard from since the war against Troy. Well, get to your benches, one on each side of the ship—you here, Tiryns, and you there, Asini—and see to it that both pull together for once. Keep the beat I set or you will finish the voyage in leg irons."

When each sat gripping his oar, ready to row, Milo took his place on deck under the eye of the captain. His flute set a brisk cadence for the two oarsmen in the hold and they thought it well to keep the beat.

There were many islands between the Peloponnese and Athens. Every night the pirates went ashore, putting the captives in leg irons and leaving two men to guard them. One of these was always Milo, who brought food and drink, finding or making other excuses to linger and talk. He had come from a decent family, he said, and had gone to school under men who were followers of the great Pythagoras, scholar of Samos. When he found that neither Alexis nor Glaukon had ever heard of him, he stayed one night and talked until dawn.

Pythagoras had left Samos for some far country, said Milo, Italy it might be, but his learning remained in Samos: the lore of numbers and how they made the whole universe move and sound in harmony, so that even the strings of the lyre responded to the divine law.

"That I know," said Alexis. "My own teacher explained it in my school at Asini."

Milo nodded. "Your teacher from Samos. Yes, he would have known. And Pythagoras taught the art of healing both the body and the mind. But there was more, much more. He said that the soul lives on, becoming more pure, or more corrupt, in each lifetime. And this was why one must be kind to slaves and to animals. He even believed that women were equal to men. He taught the beauty of excellence in all things. These ideas excited me as a boy, but I saw that there was no money to be made from them, and the life of the scholars was hard. Then one day the captain put in to our port and I happened to be there. He promised me wealth and an easy life." Milo gave a short laugh. "So I came on board. And now he owns me, body and soul."

Another night he said, "Why is it that I never hear you talking except when I am here? All the world knows that Tiryns and Asini hate each other. You were fighting when we captured you. But is your hate so important that two Greeks cannot stand together when every man's hand is against you?"

Without a look at Glaukon, Alexis burst out, "It is not only a question of Tiryns and Asini. Neleus of Tiryns committed a crime against my father. He too is a king."

Glaukon broke in. "My mother was in our ship. Do you think my father would risk her life to save your father's miserable cargo?"

"Neleus of Tiryns," said Milo, raising his eyebrows. "Without knowing the whole story, I see that we have here two young princes. All the better. If you do not bring a good price in Athens, the captain can return you to your own fathers for a princely ransom."

"You will get no ransom for me," Alexis said bitterly. "My father is already deep in debt."

"Still, I will tell the captain who you are. It may help you in some way. Meanwhile, think about old Aesop's story of the sticks. Remember, they could be broken one by one, but not when they were bound together. Forget your quarrel. Let me tell you, I hear talk in the markets everywhere. Do you know what they say about us Greeks? Half our danger is from King Darius and the other half from our own quarrels."

When Milo had gone, Glaukon said, "Let us talk about this shipwreck that you blame on my father. Do you think he does not regret it? If Tiryns and Asini were not enemies, I believe he would have come to Asini with offers of help. If your sister and I had married, the old quarrel might have ended."

"If you believe that," Alexis said, "you are a greater fool than I think. We would rather see her dead."

"Be satisfied," said Glaukon. "I will probably never see her again. But understand that we love each other. It would have been no ordinary marriage. And her life at Tiryns would have suited her. Our women are more free than yours. My mother rides with my father. She and her friends follow the hunt. And someday Niki would have been queen in my mother's place. I think you love your sister. Does all this mean nothing to you?"

Alexis was silent. Glaukon's words recalled his dreams of Niki sitting in the queen's chair at Tiryns. "Talk to Glaukon," she had said. Now they had talked, but it made no difference. Niki would never set foot in Tiryns, and Asini still had its pride, if it had nothing else.

In the morning, when Milo brought food and ordered them to the benches, he said, "Today you row together for the last time. Tonight we put in at the island of Salamis. Tomorrow is the usual day for the slave market at Athens and we cross to the port in the morning. You will wash yourselves to present a good appearance. There is a market in the port where they sell men fit only for the silver mines.

113

You had better look obedient or the captain will sell you there instead of taking you to the city market. Athenians are always eager to buy craftsmen, so they will ask what skills you have. Since you are of noble birth, you probably have no useful skills, but you have good looks and may be bought for house servants. That is your best hope. They will not ask your name or your father's name and town. When you are bought as a slave, you will be given a new name and you had better not think of the past, but accept what comes. Troublemakers fare badly. Meanwhile, try to think of any useful thing you know how to do."

He frowned at Alexis. "You are constantly touching your forehead. Leave it alone if you want it to heal."

"I have been thinking of an old slave in my family," said Alexis. "At Epidauros she heard of someone who was branded on the forehead and prayed to have the mark taken away. The priest bound it with a cloth and in the morning the mark had gone to the cloth. Some day I will go again to Epidauros."

"Don't pray for miracles," Milo answered. "The prayer not answered can leave a bitter taste. Rather, be proud of that mark. You got it trying for freedom. But pray as the Athenians do. They call on every god they know and even have statues 'to the unknown god' so that none will be offended. You had better do the same."

Phaleron, the port of Athens, struck a chill to Alexis's heart when he saw it through the morning mist of the following day. He was standing with Glaukon on the deck of the pirate ship. Their hands were bound behind them, and a length of rope linked them together. He looked for some good omen, but saw none. The bay was filled with ships whose bare masts and furled sails dipped and swayed against the gray winter sky. Beyond the ships, the shore was crowded with men shouting their wares above the din of hammers, the shrill notes of boatswains' pipes, and the braying of heavily loaded donkeys.

The captain dropped anchor in shallow water and ordered the cargo to be taken ashore. The sailors manned the small boat, returning to the ship for load after load, and spreading out their goods on the beach. When the last of the bales and jars and bundles had gone ashore, the captain returned for his prisoners. Two sailors lowered them into the boat and made the final trip to the beach. The captain stepped ashore and the sailors pushed Alexis and Glaukon after him, following at their heels.

Among pens for sheep and cattle, Alexis saw a well-filled enclosure for slaves, all of them ragged and filthy, all of them shackled. Some were clearly prisoners of war, still wearing the remnants of military tunics. Many others seemed in the last stage of long slavery, their faces brutalized, their rags barely covering the bleeding stripes of recent beatings.

As Alexis turned his eyes away, feeling cold and sick, Milo came with a bag of coins for the captain. He had sold the oxhides. Seeing the look on Alexis's face, he made a show of tightening the bonds and muttered, "You will not be sold here. I have told the captain who you are. He will sell you in the city market."

When he offered himself as a guard for the captives, the captain nodded. "You talk and sell."

Two miles inland, the horizon was crowned with the temples of the High City of Athens and Milo led the way toward it with the captain following the prisoners. The road was crowded all the way from the shops and houses of the port to a bridge over a river where a flock of sheep blocked the way. Waiting to cross the bridge, Alexis saw ahead the outlying houses of Athens, and among them, statues, countless statues. Above, very close now, were the temples of the citadel, as majestic as those at Olympia, and enclosed by walls as mighty as those at Tiryns. Fear fell upon him. Then Glaukon moved closer to him and said in a low voice, "I have prayed that the unknown god will help us."

Not "help me," but "help us." Glaukon had said it, and suddenly Alexis felt less afraid, no longer alone. He remembered Milo's words: "Forget your quarrel. We Greeks make half our troubles by our own quarrels." Too late, too late. But in this trouble that he now shared with Glaukon, should they stand together, at least until they were sold? Two sticks were harder to break than one.

They passed through a gate in the city wall and found themselves in a maze of narrow streets leading to a wider road that circled the colossal rock of the High City and was lined with the blank walls and closed doors of houses. Athens was bigger than ten Asinis, thought Alexis, trudging through city dirt and winter mud. Yet all too soon the long road opened into the marketplace, and the march came to a halt.

At the near end of a great square, Alexis saw the slave market, a circle of stone posts and ropes in which a dozen men stood shackled and ready for sale. Outside the pen a crowd of onlookers mingled with buyers, sellers, and their agents. The human goods for sale were from many foreign lands and from Greek cities as well, but at this moment, all were nameless, fatherless, homeless. They were flesh and bone for the highest bidder, nothing more.

The captain pushed his prisoners under the ropes and Milo followed them.

"What shall I say you can do?" he asked.

"I have managed my father's horses," Glaukon said.

Alexis too had thought about this problem and said that he knew farming.

Milo gave the information to the auctioneer, and came back. "They will take you in your turn. Until then, keep quiet. And if I never see you again, think of me sometimes. I will think of you." He left the ring and stood by the captain.

To avoid seeing what went on at the auction block, Alexis turned his back on it. The winter sun was breaking through the clouds and shone on handsome stone buildings and colonnades around the spacious square. Among green laurels were altars, statues, innumerable booths, and workshops. The undercurrent din of penned-up animals and poultry added to the clamor of humanity that swarmed through this space, buying and selling every sort of goods. But the high-pitched voice of the auctioneer in the slave ring penetrated all these sounds.

"Coppersmith, experienced. Trained in the best workshops of Crete. Understands enameling. Who makes an offer? . . . Yes, sir, by all means your steward may examine his hands. Of course, the owner swears that this man is in good health. You wish to see him stripped? Not young, but plenty of work left in him. Go around the ring, fellow, double time."

At the inner edge of the circle the naked man ran past, his face creased with effort and fear. The bidding ended, money changed hands, and he went away with his new master.

"Stonemason's helper. Still young and strong. Strip, and show your muscle. The brand? The owner says this man was branded ten years ago by another owner."

A voice in the crowd called, "Why was he branded?"

117

Another answered, "They said he stole food."

"Has he given trouble since then?"

"None. He is a good workman."

The auctioneer pushed the stonemason's helper from the block. "Run, and show the gentleman what you are made of." He began the bidding, which ended with a sale for a low price.

They took Glaukon. Alexis saw him on the block, his hands untied, his tunic stripped off.

"Experienced horse trainer, young and strong. Show your muscle. This man could also model for an artist. Notice the beauty of every feature."

Alexis saw Glaukon's fists clench, his brow darken. Across the heads of the crowd he looked at Alexis. Suddenly Alexis found himself praying, "Zeus, do not let him strike the auctioneer."

It was as if he had prayed against his will. He did not know how he could have uttered such a prayer. If Glaukon struck the man, they would kill him within minutes and Neleus of Tiryns would be left without an heir. There would be an end to Niki's mad dreams, and the honor of Asini would be satisfied. Yet he had prayed, returning Glaukon's look, and he saw Glaukon gain control of himself. Two sticks were indeed stronger than one. What he saw Glaukon enduring, he too could endure.

A steward pushed his way to the ring and called out an offer. It was surprisingly high, and there was no other bid. Perhaps the crowd had seen the rage in Glaukon's tensed muscles and sensed a troublemaker. His face still red with anger, he picked up his tunic and put it on. The steward paid money into Milo's hand and left the slave pen, prodding Glaukon ahead of him. Alexis lost sight of them. He prayed to Poseidon and to Asklepios. Then, remembering what Glaukon had done for him, he prayed to the unknown god. "Divine power, whoever you may be, help us." Not "help me," but "help us."

A handler seized his shoulder, propelling him to the block. The auctioneer untied his hands and stripped him. To stand naked before a crowd was nothing to Alexis, but he had never stood like an animal for sale. Shame filled his soul.

"A farmhand, young and strong. He can be taught to plough . . . to harvest. . . . Show your muscle." There were no offers. Shame was followed by despair. Who would buy a farmhand in the winter? He would be marched back to the port and sold there for the mines.

Then Alexis saw a man pushing through the crowd, the same steward who had bought Glaukon. He called out, "Why is this one branded?"

Milo hurried to the side of the steward, smiling and gesticulating, pouring out a flood of eloquence. Alexis caught the words ". . . all a mistake . . . a bargain . . . young enough to be trained to anything. Look at the legs." Milo shouted to the auctioneer, "Make him run the circle."

The handler flung Alexis his tunic, pulled him from the block, and slapped him across the buttocks to start him around the circuit of the slave pen. As he ran, he heard the steward calling out a bid. Again it was high, and again no one made another offer. Milo signaled to Alexis, counting a handful of coins into a money bag. "Sold. Go with this man," he said to Alexis. "May I ask the master's name?" he inquired of the steward with a show of friendliness.

"My master is Kimon, a gentleman and citizen of Athens."

"Where is his house?"

But it was not the steward's business to give this sort

119

of information. He pushed Alexis through the crowd to where a tall man stood with Glaukon at his side. The bearing of this man was erect, easy, and confident. His black hair and beard were neatly trimmed, his tunic was spotless white, and his white cloak was draped in careful folds. He looked from Glaukon to Alexis and said in a pleasant voice, "So Tiryns and Asini are fated to be together again."

Glaukon answered with some hesitation, but it seemed to Alexis that he spoke without fear. "You know us, then?"

"Of course," said Kimon. "I saw both of you at Olympia. I myself was a contestant in the race on horseback, though I was not fortunate enough to win. You fought in the splendid match with Dion of Asini. And you," he said to Alexis, "are Dion's young brother who won the boys' race. Both of you look older and you are very dirty, but I knew you at once."

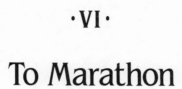

·VI·

To Marathon

·1·

KIMON spoke to the steward who had acted as his purchasing agent. "Lead the way home, Thrax. Tiryns and Asini, follow him. I trust you have too much sense to run away. I will walk behind, as rear guard."

They set off through the marketplace toward the northwest into less crowded streets. Houses still presented blank walls on each side, but the tops of the walls were bordered with painted tiles, and a bust of Hermes stood beside each doorway. Clearly, this was a desirable part of the city. Other gentlemen were returning from market with their attendants and their purchases. They exchanged cheerful greetings with Kimon and congratulated him on the good looks of his new slaves.

At the open door of a stable two horses stood in their stalls and a chariot was uptilted against a wall. A groom was sweeping litter into the street. Beyond the stable was a closed door on which the steward knocked, calling out that someone named Geta should open at once for the master. Presently the heavy door was pulled inward enough for the eye of a porter to appear in the crack. Then the door swung wide and Kimon entered with his slaves.

He tossed his cloak to the steward and said, "Geta, these boys are to have the corner room by the stable. Take

123

them to the bath as soon as possible, and then bring them to me."

The new slaves entered a bright courtyard where an altar stood, surrounded by a colonnade of yellow walls and blue columns. Rooms opened into the courtyard on both sides. Geta led the way to a room at the far end; here was the bath, a handsome basin on a tripod. Geta brought a pitcher of water from which he filled the basin, saying resentfully, "The master wants you to use his soap and towels, as if you were guests. But I am to cut your hair short and see that you are clean-shaven like any other slave. Wash your heads well. We don't want lice here. You'll have clean tunics and cloaks. Sandals, too. If they don't fit, the groom will make new ones for you tomorrow. The rest of us don't get such treatment. We wash in the stable and make our own sandals, or go without."

He worked as he talked. When he had doused them from the pitcher, he gave them a little knife to pare their nails and pointed grudgingly to a vial of good oil and a strigil for the final scraping down. "Finish and be quick about it," he said. "You are to have a meal before you see the master, and he doesn't like to be kept waiting."

When they had eaten some bread and olives, Geta led the new slaves through a dark room with gilded couches along its walls. "This is the dining hall, for the master's evening parties," he said. "Where you come from, there's nothing so fine, I suppose. Today Kimon is having lunch with the mistress and their children in the women's quarters." He knocked on a door. "You will not enter here without orders."

The door was opened by a sharp-eyed serving girl, and they passed into the second courtyard. Kimon sat at the head of his table, in the sunshine, with an elegantly dressed woman and a boy and girl who looked about the age of Alexis. All of this he took in at a glance. Then he saw that the girl's eyes were fixed on his forehead. Her eyes were dark, and her hair, tied round with a blue scarf, was as black as a raven's wing. Why then did he think of the morning star above the mountains in the bay of Asini? Having been taught not to stare at a woman, he looked down at the floor, wondering if he, a branded slave, was beneath her notice. He heard Kimon speaking, but his mind was full of this unknown girl who sat so near, this girl at whom he must not look.

"Let me come to an understanding with both of you," Kimon was saying. His voice was pleasant. "I don't intend to send you home as a present to your families, and they would not expect it. I happen to need services that you can give. But I will free you when you are no longer of use and have earned your freedom. That is my custom. It's not the custom of every master, so count yourselves lucky."

He nodded toward the woman who sat across the table from him. "This is your mistress, Petta. You will obey her orders as my own."

Alexis raised his eyes and saw a face, cool, composed, and pale as marble. The eyes were large and dark, with a quick, darting intelligence in their glance. The hair was golden, elaborately combed into curls.

Kimon spoke again. "Tiryns, you will take the place of my groom, who has bought his freedom and will be leaving this house. He will show you the duties of the stable and you will ride with me every day. Asini, you will be the pedagogue for my son Jason, responsible for his manners and his conduct. Did you have a pedagogue at home? No? The duties are important. Dromon, who has attended my son, is old. He will become Jason's personal servant, taking care of his room and his clothing. You will accompany my son to school. You will also go with him to the training ground and make a runner of him."

The boy at the table was taking the measure of the new slaves. His face was like his mother's but the curly hair and the skin were dark. His look was wary, like that of a young animal, untamed and restless.

"Listen to me, Jason," said Kimon. "You can learn a great deal from these two. Remember that they are of royal birth in their own towns. Treat them well. As for you, Asini and Tiryns, I heard at Olympia that there is no love lost between you, but give me no trouble. You owe me something."

After this day, Alexis saw little of Kimon's daughter; she was always in the women's quarters where he did not go. He learned nothing about her except that her name was Irene. When he compared her with Niki, running on the beach at Asini, wild and free, and risking her life to see his race at Olympia, this girl was almost a prisoner. Perhaps, then, she would not mind talking even to a slave, he thought. He spent most of his waking hours with Jason, but in the back of his mind was the constant hope that somehow he could find a way to talk to Irene.

He and Jason were up before dawn and on the way to school, Alexis walking behind with book, writing tablets, and lyre. The lessons were like those at Asini, but the school was bigger, and the master seemed to take no interest in the boys. He was harsh with Jason, who could handle the lyre well enough and was quick with numbers, but seldom knew his lines from Homer when he was called on to recite. He was beaten nearly every day. The other pedagogues sitting in the waiting room with Alexis were mostly older men. He took no part in their conversation but sat listening through the open door to what went on in the classroom and soon began to flinch in painful anticipation when the master called Jason's name. It was only at the training ground that both were happy. Jason showed some promise of being a good runner, and Alexis, pacing him, could remember and believe that he, a free-born Greek, had won a race at Olympia.

At the end of a week, as they made their way home from school, he did not walk behind Jason as usual, but caught up with him, asking, "Why don't you learn the lesson?"

"I can't. I can't remember the words."

"Why not? It's easy."

"When he calls my name, everything goes out of my head. My father says I don't try, but I do. He thinks I will never amount to anything."

"Do you study at night?"

"No. What's the use? Besides, there are too many people at home. I can't think there."

"Tonight, when we come back from the training ground, try to find a quiet place. There must be one somewhere."

Jason shrugged. "Only on the roof."

"On the roof, then. I'll go with you, if you want help."

Kimon and Glaukon had gone to ride and the stable was still empty in the late afternoon when Alexis and Jason climbed the stairs from the men's courtyard and stepped out onto the flat roof of the house. To the north, snow-capped mountains rimmed the horizon, and toward the west Jason pointed out the training ground where they had spent an hour in running on the practice track.

"Beyond that are the grounds where my father goes with all the men who are in training for military duty," he said. "They march and run in armor and practice with swords and spears. It's a wonderful sight."

To the south, the High City loomed on its great rock, dimly lit by the flare of altar fires among the temples. Along the distant, dark line of the shore, lights were twinkling.

"There is Phaleron, where you landed," said Jason. "Those lights to the west are on warships in the harbor and on the hill fort. I will go there for military training when I finish school."

"Will you like that?" Alexis asked.

"Better than school. My father was there when he was young."

"It's getting late. We should begin," said Alexis.

They sat down on the roof, their backs against the low parapet. The lesson for the next day was about the fall of Troy and was so splendid that Alexis thought there could be no trouble in learning it by heart; Telamon had taught it to him easily. But Jason could not remember even the first words.

"It's about Hector leaving Troy," Alexis prompted. " 'He put the boy in the hands of his dear wife . . .' "

" 'He put the boy in the hands . . . of his wife . . .' " Jason faltered. "Oh, I can't do it."

"You can. See it as if it were happening. Hector is the greatest of the Trojan heroes, remember? He's going out from Troy to fight against the Greeks. His wife runs to the city gate with their little boy and begs him to think what will happen to her and the child if Hector is killed. He says he knows this, and it's a terrible thought. He even knows that Troy will fall. But he must go. When he wants to take his son in his arms, the baby is frightened by the bronze helmet, and cries. Hector takes off the helmet and kisses the child and gives him back to the mother. Now do you remember the words?"

Jason shook his head.

"Listen," said Alexis. " 'He put the boy in the hands of his dear wife, and she, smiling through her tears, took him to her sweet breast. Her husband pitied her and caressed her, saying, "Dear one, do not grieve too much for me. No man can send me to death until my time comes. But no one escapes death, neither the coward nor the brave man. Go home to your weaving and spinning, and set your serving girls to work too. The men will see to the war, I most of all the Trojans." ' " Alexis paused. "It might be your father and mother, or mine, saying goodbye, if our cities were at war."

"Yes," said Jason, "it is fine, as you say it. And it might be my father. Not my mother."

Alexis asked no questions, but led Jason through the passage, line by line, and this time it went well.

He learned more about the mistress of the house from the young serving girl whom he had first seen at the door of the women's quarters. She was old beyond her years, and her mistress called her Echo because she talked so much. She often came to fill the men's pitchers with water from the well in the women's courtyard. Jason's old pedagogue, now his servant, gave the young master's tunics to her for mending and washing, and when she brought them back, she always lingered to talk to the new slaves as long as she dared. One day she told them she had been a foundling, left as a baby on the steps of an altar.

"It was a shrine to Demeter and Persephone, the Great Mother and her child; I suppose it was a good place to leave babies. Kimon found me there and brought me home. He is kind, you know. We are not beaten or branded. If we are lazy, he threatens to sell us, but he never does. Petta let me stay because I would grow up as one more slave to wait on her. She sits in her room thinking of work for all of us to do."

"Does she do no work herself?" asked Alexis, remembering home, where Melissa's work never seemed to stop.

"Work? No, indeed. Irene, the daughter, does it all. Petta sleeps late. Then we bathe her and touch up the roots of her hair—she is as dark as her children, really—and we do her curls, three or four times over. It is noon before she has chosen her tunic and the perfume and pins and rings and necklaces to go with it. After lunch she takes a nap so that she won't look old and tired when the master comes home."

Glaukon too was remembering a different way of life. "In Tiryns, my mother manages the household and cares for all the people, even the slaves, if they are sick. Who does that for you?"

"Irene takes care of us," said Echo.

"Doesn't your mistress go out for exercise or pleasure? What does she have to think about?"

"Oh, sometimes when there are festivals, she goes up on the roof with the rest of us to look down at the processions in the street. She visits her women friends, and they come here sometimes to gossip. She loves gossip. And she watches what we do and starts quarrels among us, just for the excitement. She makes little plots to see what will happen. Watch out. She is interested in you two because you are different from the rest of us."

Before spring something happened that changed Alexis's life. He and Jason were on the roof one evening, the parapet at their backs, warmed by the setting sun. As they worked on the next day's lesson, they heard a girl's voice singing. Jason jumped up and ran to the back of the roof where a flight of stairs led up from a walled garden. "Irene, come up," he called. "Yes, you can. It's lovely up here. Never mind your work. The gardener can do it without you."

A moment later, Kimon's daughter came up the steps, smiling and rubbing garden soil from her hands. Her dark hair was gathered under a net and a heavy apron covered her tunic. Her cheeks were flushed with working in the cool fresh air.

"I mustn't stay," she said, breathlessly. She spoke only to her brother, avoiding Alexis's eyes. "They will be wanting me."

"You do too much," said Jason. "See how fine the High City is at this time of day, as if it were built of gold. And look north. The snow on the mountains seems on fire."

Irene shaded her eyes, gazing all around the horizon. "There's a little green on the hills," she said. "Before long, old King Pluto will let Persephone come back to us and it will be spring. Do you remember the story, Jason? And look at Hymettus, turning violet. In this light you can almost see how the thyme covers it. The bees will soon be at work there, and we'll have honey again."

Melissa, thought Alexis. This girl made him think of home and all that he loved there. Melissa, and the bee making honey. Irene did not look at him and she seemed to be only thinking aloud when she spoke again, pointing toward the foot of the High City. "Somewhere over there is the altar to Asklepios. Once my father took me to the High City and offered sacrifices to the god. I wish I could see his statue and the great serpent."

"The serpent that is the god?" said Alexis. "He lives under a mound at Epidauros. I have been there and I know."

131

"I have heard of that too," said Irene. "If I could choose, I would go to Epidauros or some other temple of Asklepios and learn to serve the god and to heal." She turned to Jason. "When my herbs are ready for picking, I will make a wreath for him. Will you take it to his altar for me?"

She made no secret of this meeting, and to the surprise of Alexis, the mistress seemed to encourage other meetings between them. When Kimon wanted Jason to have riding lessons from Glaukon, Petta sent Alexis to work with Irene in the garden. She allowed Irene to come to the roof when Alexis was there with Jason. She even called Alexis to the women's courtyard to entertain her with passages from Homer, accompanying himself on the lyre. She asked for all the lines about beautiful women and goddesses who held men captive or brought them to their death. And when he had sung all he knew of these, she showed him her pet monkey who did tricks, and a bird that hopped about, tied to a string. Irene was usually in the courtyard, busy at some task, weaving or spinning with the slave girls, or at work with her flowers and herbs. As spring came on, the courtyard was filled with sweet and spicy scents while Irene mixed lotions and ointments or wove blossoms and flowers into wreaths for the city altars where her father went to offer sacrifice.

One night Alexis dreamed about Irene. He saw her in the courtyard at Asini, moving to and fro before a loom and singing softly to herself as she worked. There was a fragrance, perhaps from scented wood that burned on the hearth, perhaps from a wreath of flowers that Irene wore on her hair, and he knew that she was waiting for him to come. He woke happier than he had ever been in his life and feeling that he must talk to someone. Had he had a true dream? There was no one to talk to but Glaukon.

Since their last conversation on the pirate ship, ending in a quarrel about Niki, they had exchanged words only when necessary. At night they shared their room as if in an armed truce, and in the morning they went their separate ways. Yet Alexis remembered that they had prayed for each other in the hands of the slave traders, and since then, something in him had changed. Often, lying awake in the dark room, dimly lit by torches in the men's courtyard, he looked at Glaukon, wrapped in his cloak, silent and still on his cot, and the sight no longer filled him with the old smoldering rage and resentment that he had nursed all the years of his life. He and Glaukon had been through the worst together and he had found Glaukon unfailing in courage and honor. He decided to speak.

It was hard to break through the barrier of silence that had lasted for so long between them, but the morning after his dream he said to Glaukon, "The daughter of the house is very good."

"Yes, very good."

"And beautiful. Have you noticed her eyes? Her hair? Her hands?"

"No," said Glaukon, smiling. "But you have. I have seen you watching her. It is Niki who makes me feel like that. Now it seems the boy with the arrows has knocked on your door too, and you have let him in."

"So you know Niki's little song," said Alexis. "I never really understood it before. It's true that the arrows hurt."

"You are too young to marry," Glaukon said.

Alexis knew it. There were other difficulties too. Though his father was king in Asini, he was poor, and Alexis was not even the oldest son. In Athens, he was the lowest of the low, a branded slave. But he would be free again some day, and in the meantime, he had noticed Irene's mother smiling as she watched them together. She must think well of him. As for Kimon, after the first day he treated Alexis like his other slaves, showing no special favors, calling him "Asini" or "boy," as if he had no other name. Yet Kimon had seen him winning a victory at Olympia as a free-born Greek. Nothing could change that, and surely Kimon would remember it when the time came for him to choose a husband for Irene.

"If she will wait for me, I too can wait," thought Alexis.

· 2 ·

The festival of Dionysus came. The streets were filled with crowds, dancing, singing, drinking, their heads crowned with flowers. At dawn of the third day, Kimon and Jason went to the theater of Dionysus to see a play, while the household waited for their return and prepared the dining hall for a party. Couches were moved out from the wall and spread with embroidered covers; sconces were filled with new torches, ready for lighting. The painted floor was washed and polished. Kimon would bring choice fish, fruit, and vegetables from the market place. Glaukon was to help the steward in mixing the wine. Alexis worked with the gardener, cutting branches of laurel for the dining hall. Irene and Echo sat in the shade of the garden wall, plaiting wreaths for the guests.

"They say Dionysus loves violets," said Irene, "and our city is called 'the violet-crowned,' so we honor Athens too. Does your town celebrate as we do?"

"In a simpler way," said Alexis. "The people wear

wreaths and get drunk, but there is no theater and there are no dinner parties like this. Everything at Asini is simpler."

Irene sent Echo and the gardener into the house with flowers and branches, saying, "I will come to help you later." When they had gone, she said to Alexis, "Tell me about your family."

"There is my brother, the Olympic boxer, and my sister, who is about your age. My grandfather has died, but my grandmother is still living, besides my father and mother. They must wonder whether I am still alive. My father is king in Asini."

"Where is his house?"

"It is an old palace, built before the Greeks sailed for Troy. Eighty ships went from our part of Greece, all led by Diomedes. He was the hero the Trojans feared most of all. Our palace stands on a cliff above the bay. There are islands, and there are mountains all around. We pray to Poseidon. In the spring, when I was at home, I saw the morning star over the mountains."

"It must be very beautiful," she said. "I wish that I could see your home."

Scarcely able to believe his own happiness, he answered, "I have dreamed that you were there."

Before he could say more, voices were raised in the kitchen.

"My father must have come with the special cook," Irene said. "Now our own cook will be in a temper. I'm needed in the kitchen."

Kimon appeared in the garden doorway, saying, "So there you are, boy. I shall want you and Jason to serve the guests tonight. Jason has served before and can tell you what to do. Also, I want him to sing and play for the guests. I'm pleased with his progress since you have been working with him. Help him to choose something short, but worthy of the occasion. There will be six guests, all friends who take military training with me, and the guest of honor is a poet and playwright as well as a patriot. We saw one of his plays this morning. His name is Aeschylus."

Alexis was startled. "I know his name. My teacher heard him reciting his verses at Olympia and taught me one of them."

Kimon smiled. "Recite it for us tonight. Aeschylus is an actor himself, so do your best. Ask Geta for a fresh tunic and comb your hair over your forehead. You will look very well."

That afternoon, in their place of retreat on the roof, Alexis recommended that Jason should give the guests the lines from Homer where Odysseus speaks to his son as they stand shoulder to shoulder against their enemies. In return, Jason told Alexis how they should serve the guests. "As each man comes, we go to his couch and untie his shoes or sandals. We bring bowls of water and towels to wash and dry their feet, and more fresh water for their hands. Then they settle back on their couches and we bring the food from the kitchen in the best silver bowls and cups. There are little tables to go in front of the couches and we must not knock them over or drop anything. We don't speak unless they ask us a question. When we have cleared the tables and swept the floor, the guests sing the hymn to Apollo and we bring in the dessert and the wreaths. We sing for them and go. Then some real musicians will come, and dancing girls, and older women who are professional entertainers. We'll hear them laughing and singing and drinking until late."

As evening came on, the guests arrived. Alexis worked with Jason in the dining hall and listened to the talk which seemed to flash about the room from one man to another, sparked by the presence of the honored guest. Aeschylus was not a big man, but his voice, the trained voice of an actor, carried over and through all other voices. His body, even as he lay relaxed on his couch, had a look of controlled energy. How long had it been since the games at Olympia when Alexis had first heard of this poet? "His name is Aeschylus," Telamon had said. "If you run across him, listen."

Dinner ended with platters of apples and grapes, almonds, and honey cakes. Alexis and Jason brought a wreath for each guest, Glaukon filled a great bowl with wine and water, and Kimon poured a libation to Zeus the Protector. Then the guests sang the hymn to Apollo and the real event of the evening began.

"A toast to Aeschylus and his poetry," said Kimon, looking round the circle. "He will be master of ceremonies for tonight and choose our subject."

He raised his cup. The toast was drunk with a round of applause, which Aeschylus acknowledged with a smile.

"My verses are only slices from Homer's feast," he said. "But for our conversation tonight, let me tell you about a dream that has come to me many times. I see two beautiful women, one Greek, one Persian, but sisters, of one blood. They quarrel, and the son of King Darius appears, trying to gentle them, as a charioteer gentles two spirited horses to pull his chariot. The Persian accepts the yoke, but the Greek will not bear it and tears it away, so that the king's son falls. Then he sees his father's ghost and cries out in shame and anguish. This is my dream. Shall we talk about it and see if it has meaning? Or is the subject too serious for a festive evening like this?"

"It is serious," Kimon said, "but these are serious times. Shall I speak first? Your beautiful Greek woman, let

137

us call her Athens, because we will have to fight alone, if the Persians attack again."

The guests spoke one after another, ideas pouring out with emotion.

"Not *if* the Persians attack, but *when* they attack. Ever since we went to relieve Miletus and burned Sardis, Darius has sworn revenge on Athens. We know that. They say a servant tells him each day, on orders, 'Remember the Athenians.' "

"And Eretria?"

"He will not forget Eretria."

"But here's an amusing story. I'm told that he has sent spies to find out what we are like. When he heard that our soldiers are ordinary citizens who also do business and play the lyre and dance and attend the theater in our leisure time, he was certain that we were soft, an easy conquest."

This brought a general laugh before the conversation went on.

"What can he know—an absolute monarch who rules by torture and the lash? Imagine his opinion of a city that makes its decisions by debating and persuading, a city that has no ruler but the law. He must think we are insane."

"Perhaps he is right. No one claims that democracy is a simple way to govern. It may fail. But we have had kings, both good and bad; we have been ruled by good and bad tyrants, and the last one was the worst. Before we got rid of him, Athens was no more valiant than any other city. But no sooner did we shake off the yoke than we became the first city of Greece. And why? Because now each man knows that when he fights for his city, he is fighting for himself and his family."

"As for tyrants, we have expelled Hippias, but are we

really rid of him? Since he fled to the court of Darius and is still there, it's certain that when Darius comes, Hippias will be with him, ready to be tyrant in Athens again."

"And if your dream is true, Aeschylus, not only must we fight Darius, but our sons must some day fight his son, Xerxes."

"That is what I believe," said Aeschylus. "Freedom is like love. It has to be won over and over. You know the saying, 'After every victory the victor's wreath fades and there is always another contest to be faced.' "

"But can we really oppose Darius? To the north, the south, and the east, the world is his. We are one small corner to the west, and even in Athens there are some who want to ask for peace and accept Hippias as tyrant."

"How many great cities Darius has brought down in ruins! He can raise armies and navies everywhere. What is our navy? Seventy ships at the most. And how many men can we muster for our infantry?"

"Perhaps ten thousand," said Kimon, "if you mean men fully trained and armed. But even the poorest citizens, even without armor, would volunteer, I think. Free men can fight with sticks and stones, if need be. With a slave, light-armed, for each soldier, we would have twenty-five thousand."

Several voices broke in.

"Against ten times as many Persians."

"Can we count on any allies? Would Sparta come?"

"She has fought Persia when it served her purpose, and there are no better soldiers, by Heracles. But Sparta always has her own point of view."

"What Greek city doesn't have its own point of view? It seems we can only agree every four years at Olympia."

"Old Aesop was wiser than the rest of us," said

Aeschylus, smiling. "If we could only remember his story of the sticks that became strong when they were tied into one bundle!"

The dubious one spoke again. "If only! But think how many fools we have in this city. And how many are faint-hearted."

"I too am a fool and faint-hearted at times," Aeschylus answered. "Yet when I put on my breastplate and helmet, I am like an actor putting on his mask. I become something more than myself. I stand for an idea. And now when our country is in mortal danger, I see that Greece too is more than the place where we live. With all its faults, it stands for an idea and is more than itself, just as the shield of Achilles was more than a shield. It stood for Greece. We will fight for that idea."

"And our casualties?"

"There speaks our doctor. You think that Athens is a hopeless case, Andreas? Are you saying that we should sue for peace?"

"Never. I think we should fight. But our doctors should be prepared."

Kimon spoke. "Suppose we offer to free any slave who offers to stand with us, not as a slave serving his master, but as a fighting man like any other citizen?"

Alexis, standing in the shadows, began to listen intently.

There was silence, then a dubious voice. "It has never been done."

Another man raised an objection. "With all due respect, Kimon, many Greek cities and many of the islands have surrendered to Darius, sometimes without a struggle. Is Athens so different from all others?"

"To surrender to tyranny without a struggle, that is

not Greek," said Aeschylus. "The Greek spirit means freedom, not slavery."

"We say these things, yet we own Greek slaves."

"Some day we will free all our slaves. And what is a slave? Slavery can happen to anyone, for many reasons. In some of our cities there is still slavery for debt. That could happen to the best of men. There are slaves who were foundlings, prisoners of war, and those taken by pirates. The body may be enslaved, but if the desire for liberty is alive, the mind is free."

Suddenly Aeschylus seemed to remember the presence of the two young slaves in the dining hall. "This is not the time or the place for such talk, Kimon. You will curse me for sounding such a grim note in the harmony of your dinner party. I give the evening back to our host."

Calling on Glaukon to refill the cups, Kimon said, "I agree, it is time to restore harmony. Gentlemen, you have been served this evening by my son Jason and by two young men whose adventures would rival those of Odysseus, if we could hear them, but their story must wait. If any of you were at Olympia last summer, you may recognize them. It was there that this boy Asini heard a poem by our guest of honor." At his nod, Alexis took his place, facing Aeschylus, and struck the first notes of his melody, praying that his memory and his voice would not fail him.

> "*An eagle, struck by an arrow from a bow,*
> *Said, when he saw the winged traitor,*
> '*So, not by others but by our own plumes*
> *We're taken.*' "

There was generous applause and praise. "Beautiful . . ." "The boys' race . . ." "Very good form . . ." "A bright future . . ." He blushed with surprise and relief.

141

Aeschylus smiled at him. "An excellent performance of my simple verse. Now tell us the meaning of old Aesop's fable."

Alexis was not prepared for this. "At Olympia," he answered, hesitating, "it was told to me because of the accident in the chariot race. My teacher said that the accident was the price of a rich man's dangerous sport."

Aeschylus nodded. "A good answer, but not the whole answer. We should talk again some day, you and I."

"My son Jason may not do as well," said Kimon, "but he has learned a few lines for your pleasure."

"You will do well," Alexis said under his breath. "Think of the meaning and look only at your father."

Jason picked up the lyre, his fingers trembling. He glanced desperately around the circle of strange faces. Then he looked into his father's face and began to sing: "Odysseus spoke to his dear son and said, 'Telemachus, when you come to the place of battle, where the best men fight, do not bring shame on your father's house or on us who in time past have been famous for strength and courage in all the world.' Then wise Telemachus answered, 'Dear father, it will be as you have said. Watch me and you will see that I shall not disgrace my family.' "

Kimon only nodded to dismiss the performers, but the applause brought tears to his eyes.

When they had left the hall, Jason said, "Tonight, for the first time in my life, I really pleased my father. Thank you, Alexis."

Waiting in the men's courtyard were a flute boy, a girl with a basket full of knives, and two women dressed in brighter colors than any good woman would wear. They went quickly into the dining hall and the door closed behind them.

Alexis lay awake late, listening to the talk and laughter and the sound of metal clanging. He heard singing, first the voices of men, then a woman with a song about spells and charms to hold a lover captive. He thought of the mistress, Petta, with her little tethered bird, and wondered if she was listening from the women's courtyard.

When the guests had gone at last, Glaukon told him how the party had ended. "Each one sang a song to honor Dionysus. The girl set up her knives in a circle and danced through them, in and out. I was amazed."

"And the women?" asked Alexis.

"They sat on the couches with the men. There were riddles and other games. There was kissing. Do you remember the man who said that you were beautiful? He is an artist and asked Kimon if he would allow you to pose for him some day. At the end, Kimon balanced a bronze bowl on a spindle and all of them were throwing wine to knock it off."

Alexis tried to picture such a scene. Athens was indeed a different world from Asini, or from Tiryns. His grandfather had said that he would go far from home, and it had come true. He had come far not only in distance but in experience. No one here but Glaukon would understand what he felt. Staring through the dark toward the corner where Glaukon lay on his cot, Alexis thought, "I still hate his father. Nothing can change that, but it is not Glaukon's fault. How easy it is to talk to him now, and what became of the hatred I used to feel toward him?" Then he remembered the old saying:

> *What we look for does not come to pass;*
> *The gods find a way that we did not expect.*

Niki had said it almost a year ago when she heard it from a fortuneteller at Olympia. And it too was a true saying.

On the day after Kimon's dinner party, Echo found Alexis in the men's courtyard, retuning Jason's lyre. "You should stop thinking about Irene," she said, and sat down beside him.

He felt his face growing hot. "I am not thinking about her."

"Of course you are. Everyone knows it. But there is no chance for you, none at all."

He stopped fingering the strings. "How do you know that?"

"Last night Kimon arranged Irene's marriage to Andreas, the doctor. Today the mistress told me that they have been talking about it for months. The only question was the dowry, and now that is settled."

Alexis burst out, "But Andreas is almost as old as Kimon."

"That is how they want it to be," Echo said. "It is the best way, so they say. He knows a great deal, you see, and can teach her what he wants her to know."

Alexis was silent.

Echo put her hand on his shoulder. "A moment ago, your face was scarlet. Now it is as pale as marble. I am sorry for you, Asini. Did you really think that you could marry Kimon's daughter?"

"Her mother made me think so," he muttered.

"Yes, she encouraged you. I saw her smiling when you were with Irene. And all the while, she knew about Andreas. I did not know, or I would have warned you. She was only making one of her little plots to amuse herself,

144

and now she will watch to see what happens next. Why don't you think of me, instead, Asini? We could be happy together, and no one would object."

He shook his head. "Too late."

She watched him quietly, but since he did not speak again, she sighed and went away.

· 3 ·

For hundreds of years the family of Kimon had owned a farm in the hills north of Athens, and as summer came on, he sent Jason there with Alexis and Glaukon.

"I must be here on military training all summer," he said. "Thrax will go to be in charge, but you will have more freedom in the country. The roads will give you good conditions for distance running, and I keep horses there for riding. In your spare time you can all lend a hand with the farm work. A change from school will be good for you, Jason. When I was your age I learned to drive a straight furrow; it puts muscles on your arms and shoulders. And if Hesiod is right, the gods bless only those who do useful work."

They set off before dawn the following morning, all in good spirits except for the steward, Thrax, who had had a hard life in Thrace, his northern homeland, and much preferred Athens.

"Your father wants you to understand the farm thoroughly," he said to Jason. "Sheep, goats, horses, poultry, garden, orchard, vineyard, fields, you are to learn everything. You won't be idle. Nor will I," he added grimly.

"I know what my father wants," said Jason. "He is

afraid I might grow up wasting my time with women and gambling and cock fighting, sleeping late every day. But don't worry, Thrax. The farm isn't like school. You won't have to make me work."

"And you, Tiryns, I must say you are in luck," Thrax went on. "Kimon's horses are champions. He bought them at Elis last summer before the Games. Riding and racing, it's just what you like. And then, you and Asini are country fellows."

"You know very little about the Peloponnese," said Glaukon shortly. "But everyone knows that Thrace is full of simple-minded people like you, wild men and barbarians."

Jason laughed, looking around with pleasure, and said, "It's a pity that Irene couldn't come. She loves the country. But my mother says there is too much work to be done at home, new clothes for all of us, and other things that women do before a wedding."

Alexis was glad to have left Irene behind him. Now that she was hopelessly out of his reach, it was best not to see her at all. Yet he thought of her as they stopped at the top of a hill to look back on the High City and the roofs of houses clustered around it. The dawn was coming up over Hymettus where Irene said the bees gathered honey. In the dim distance he could see the ships riding at anchor in the bay. Phaleron! And after Phaleron had come the slave market, and Kimon, and Irene. How strange the journey had been. More than anything in the world he had wanted to go home to Asini and to find it all unchanged. But now he himself had changed. Asini was still home and the old love was as strong as ever, but Asini was part of something beyond its own walls. Olympia, Tiryns, Epidauros, Athens, they too were part of his homeland. And now he did not know whether his road would lead him back to Asini or on to some place still unguessed.

As they walked on, Alexis remembered his dream at Epidauros. He had seen a bay filled with ships. They were not Greek ships and the bay was not Asini nor Phaleron. The good priest Laos had said, "The thing that you expect will not happen, but the god will show you the way. At the end of your road the shield of Achilles will be in your hand and you will be that shield." Where would he find the end of his road?

On this day it was leading him north through a river valley watered by streams that came down from the mountains. The road wound through gray-green olive groves and orchards where apples and pears were ripening. Sheep grazed in pastures along the river. Scarlet poppies dotted the gold of the wheat fields.

"It doesn't feel so strange here," Glaukon said. "It looks like home."

"Would you fight for it?" asked Thrax. "Ever since the dinner party in the spring, when Aeschylus came, the master has been expecting an attack from Persia. The last time they came, we barbarians, as you call us, bore the brunt of it in Thrace."

"I would fight for myself, to be free," said Glaukon. "But who knows where the Persians would land?"

Alexis said, "My teacher told me a year ago that Darius would be at Athens one day and at Asini the next. It all seemed far away then."

"I would fight if I could," said Jason. "This summer, teach me to throw the javelin."

No one laughed or told him that he was too young. "At least you will know how to ride," Glaukon said. "If you do well, we'll try a torch race."

"And every day a distance run," said Alexis. "I'm a sprinter, so I have something to learn too. It will make soldiers of us."

Before noon they came within sight of the farm. Jason pointed ahead. "There it is! There it is! I will beat you to the gate. Race with us, Glaukon." He kicked off his sandals and began to run.

From that day, Alexis ran for miles on the country roads with Jason and Glaukon. He threw himself into the work on the farm, willingly joining the laborers in the fields, the vineyards, and the orchards where they were picking the first apples of the season. He put Irene out of his mind until one day when they were resting at noon under the shade of apple trees at the edge of a wheat field. He slept and saw Irene bending over him, her arms filled with poppies. She gave him a handful of flowers and then went away. When he woke, his fingers were closed around a few poppies that grew among the wheat. He did not know whether Irene had really come to him or whether it was only a false dream from the gates of ivory, but he remembered that a medicine was made from poppies to ease pain; Peteos, the young priest, had told him so at Epidauros. And now he was curiously comforted, as if a wound had been healed.

Until the end of the summer Alexis felt more free than he had ever felt. To run, to hurl a javelin and see it arching against the stainless blue of the sky, to sweat under the sun, working until his muscles ached, this was happiness enough. He had never laughed so much. Sometimes at night he watched Jason and Glaukon, stripped and riding bareback along the road at a gallop, managing the reins with the left hand only. In their right hands they held torches high above their heads, and Glaukon taught Jason

148

to pass and catch a torch as they rode. The flames streamed backward in the darkness, blotting out the stars.

One day all three ran north through the hills and turned east to swim in the blue bay of Marathon. Dark mountains rose on the far side of the water.

"Eretria is over there," said Jason. "My father says they will be wanting our help if the Persians come."

When Kimon judged that Jason should return to school and sent for them to come back to Athens, they ran the whole distance from the farm to the city gate.

Kimon was now leaving his house early every day for the training ground, his breastplate and greaves flashing as he stepped into the light. When he pulled on his helmet and mounted his horse, it was hard to remember that a good-natured face was hidden behind the fearsome metal that covered it. Glaukon walked with him, carrying the heavy shield and spear.

Once more Alexis took up his duties as Jason's pedagogue, walking behind him each morning to school with his lyre and slate. On such a morning soon after their return, they had reached the door of the school when Alexis saw coming toward him a bearded man, who stared at him open-mouthed. The beard was so thick and full that it covered all the face but the eyes and nose, yet he knew the voice when the man cried out, "Alexis! Alexis!" and elbowed through the crowd to embrace him. Jason watched in amazement.

"Alexis," the man said, his voice breaking with emotion, "I hardly knew you. Following some pupil like a poor pedagogue? And a scar on your forehead. What has happened to you? We must talk."

Alexis returned the embrace. "Jason, go in to school," he said. "I have found an old friend. This is Telamon, the

149

teacher who taught me all that I've taught you. I will come back for you."

He went with Telamon to the marketplace where they found a bench among the stalls of the hucksters.

"There is too much to tell," Alexis began. "I was taken by pirates and branded when I tried to escape. They sold me here. Glaukon of Tiryns is with me under the same master."

Telamon groaned, looking at Alexis's forehead.

"No, don't look so angry," said Alexis. "Kimon is a good man and I am sure we will be freed when the son comes of age. Meanwhile I have learned many things that are worth knowing. I have even met the great Aeschylus. At Olympia you told me that I might learn something from him some day."

"It is a pity you could not have learned to keep out of trouble," said Telamon. "Your family only know that your grandfather's sword and spear were gone, and they found signs of a fight on the beach at Tiryns. I have just come from Asini, and they told me how fearful they have been for you. Do you wonder why I went back to the place where I had been a slave? I couldn't resist going back as a free man. I tried Samos first, but Samos is too close to Asia for comfort these days, and silversmithing with my father did not suit me. But Asini was not for me, either. The town had found another teacher, and I had always meant to go to Athens—so, here I am."

"And my family?" Alexis asked. "Are they well? Has Melissa's child been born?"

"A fine baby boy, well and strong, whom they have called Alexis for your sake, thinking that you might never return. Melissa lets no one nurse him but herself, and he is fed honey too, you can be sure. Gorgo spoils him, and old Chrysis adores him because he is another Alexis."

"And Niki, and Dion? Tell me about his eyes."

Telamon hesitated, then said, "Dion works hard. He can see enough to do all your father could wish. Niki is more beautiful than ever, but very sad for you, and even more for Glaukon. She said little about him, you know, but those things can't be kept secret in a family. She won't give up hope that you will all come back."

Alexis paled. "All? What do you mean?"

"I have to tell you, Alexis, that your father left home on a voyage soon after the birth of the child. It was a trading voyage, but he would be looking for you, too, as he has done ever since you went away. When I left Asini, he had been gone for three months, and nothing had been heard of him."

"I must go back!" Alexis cried. "Yet how can I? I owe something to Kimon, as he said. Well, at least I must get word to Asini. I know they cannot ransom me, but they must know that I am alive and will come back. Can you go again?"

Telamon shook his head. "I am starting a school for a few boys whose fathers have already paid my fee. But I will let you know if I find someone to take a message to your family. Meanwhile, Alexis, you still sound like the rash, impulsive boy I knew at Asini. Do not try to escape. A runaway slave is at the mercy of every villain."

They sat talking all the morning and parted with a promise to watch for each other.

"We may meet here again," said Alexis, "and I think that Kimon would allow you to come to his house." But after that day they did not meet. Weeks passed with no news from Telamon.

Once more Petta set Alexis to work in the garden and

151

the women's courtyard, but the arrow no longer twisted in his heart when he saw Irene among the garden herbs or sitting with her head bent over the embroidery for her wedding robes. He saw that she had given herself to the new life she was about to enter, and Echo said that Irene was happy.

"Her father has made a good choice for her. Andreas cannot help falling in love with her and he has promised to teach her all that she wants to learn about healing. What could be better? Have you put her out of your mind, Asini?" She looked at him out of the corner of her eye.

He had not quite done that. Because of Irene, he would heal Niki's pain if he could. Somehow he would help Glaukon return to her.

On a warm evening of early autumn, Alexis talked to Irene for the last time. Except for Petta, who said she had a headache and made Echo stay with her, Kimon's entire household had gathered on the roof to watch the crowds below. For several days, the streets had been full of men and women wearing white cloaks. Now they were moving toward the western gate and beyond it along the Sacred Way, chanting as they went. Alexis was standing with the other servants when he found Irene at his side.

"Do you know this festival, Alexis?" she asked. "It is the greatest one of all the year in Athens. You do not celebrate the Great Mysteries at Asini? They honor the Earth Mother, Demeter, and her daughter, the Maiden, Persephone. The people have brought the ancient statues from Eleusis, on the other side of the hills, where Demeter first planted corn and fruit and flowers. Anyone can go, slaves too. They have bathed in the sea to be purified, and they have slept and dreamed to bring the Holy Ones close. Now they are taking the statues back to Eleusis for the Mysteries."

The sleep and the dreaming, Alexis thought to himself. Like Epidauros. "What happens at Eleusis?" he asked.

"I only know that when night comes, they carry torches. You will see them soon. After the torches go out, everything is dark and secret and terrible. Then comes a wonderful light, and great joy and harmony. It must be like dying and coming to life again, as Persephone does each year when she has spent the winter under the dark earth and returns to our world in the springtime."

Behind them a man's voice said, "There speaks the gardener."

Alexis turned and saw Andreas, who had joined them quietly while they talked. He was looking down at Irene and smiling. "I take comfort in that story," he went on. "We poor doctors would raise the dead if we could, but Zeus did not allow even Asklepios to do that. We must be thankful that the gods bring back the spring without our help. See, the torches."

Along the Sacred Way the stream of people poured like a river of fire toward Eleusis. Andreas talked gently to Irene and she gave him fleeting glances of trust and admiration. Then Echo was tapping Irene's shoulder and Alexis heard, "The mistress says you must come to her. You too, sir, if you will."

Andreas went away with Irene. Presently the roof was empty except for Alexis, who stood alone looking out toward the Sacred Way until the light of the torches faded behind the hills and he could no longer hear the sound of the chanting.

The next morning, Kimon, fully armed, strode into the men's courtyard and called, "Tiryns! Asini! I have new work for you. Follow me." Walking rapidly, he led them to the stable, where he mounted his horse, saying, "Carry my

153

spear, Tiryns, and keep up with me, both of you." He went on talking as he rode. "Jason must do without you. Dromon can take him to school again as he used to do, and there will be no more riding for me except at the training ground. You will learn your duties there."

They ran beside Kimon's horse all the way, following streets where other citizen soldiers, mounted or on foot, were hurrying in the same direction. The training ground, east of the city, was already filled with more armed men than Alexis had ever seen. Each had come with one or two slaves to carry spears or the master's heavy shield, but none were armed themselves. That day the slaves learned why they had been brought here and what lay ahead for them.

Darius, lord of all men from the rising to the setting sun, was now gathering the mightiest armies ever known and was about to send them against Athens and Eretria. Warships and transports for horses were being built in all the coastal cities of the Persian empire. The Athenians could expect to be overwhelmed by land and by sea if they did not send Darius earth and water as a sign of submission, agreeing to have Hippias again as tyrant. Word had spread through the city that the attack might come soon; Kimon had heard it from Andreas the previous night.

Friends and neighbors who took their training together would fight shoulder to shoulder. "We will be ready to repulse archers, mounted or on foot," said Kimon. "For this first day, watch, and keep out of the way. Later you will be trained to follow the armed infantry in skirmishes. If we were defeated in time of war, you would take part in a delaying action. If we win, you will pursue the enemy. You will be armed with sword and spear and a wicker shield equal to what the Persians have. I do not force you to fight. When the attack comes, you can choose to stay here. But if you serve in the action, wherever it may be, you will go with me as free men."

The two exchanged glances. Then Glaukon said, "We will go with you."

Kimon took them to the Street of the Armorers where masters were buying weapons for their slaves and the poorer citizens bargained for what they could afford: swords with broken handles, spears lacking the shaft, battered wicker shields. At the door of every shop, business was brisk. Alexis recognized men he had seen at Kimon's house. He saw Aeschylus, who was buying the best he could find for a younger brother. Kimon bought two strong new shields, leather caps, and an armful of javelins.

"Now for the swords," he said. "Choose the right size to fit your hand."

At a table covered with old swords Alexis stood trying the feel of the handles in his grasp. One of them fitted as if it had been made for him. He looked at the handle and saw the letter Alpha.

"Alpha . . . Abas! I have found my grandfather's sword!" he cried out, and showed it to Kimon. "The pirates took it on the beach at Tiryns, and here it is!"

"Alpha stands for Athens, too," said Kimon, feeling the sword for weight. "All our weapons are marked with the letter. But have it. If it is not your grandfather's sword, you have found another as good. Tiryns, you will want something heavier. If you survive, you can take your swords home as a present from me." Alpha might stand for Athens, but Alexis felt that the gods had put Abas's sword into his hand again.

Throughout the winter, training continued for Glaukon and Alexis as well as for Kimon. They were under the command of a citizen named Miltiades, a man with muscles and nerves of iron, and a voice like a trumpet blast. Then came the week of Irene's wedding and Kimon got leave from training for himself and his slaves. The house was full of guests and there was extra work for all to do.

The courtyards were hung with green garlands; urns were filled with flowers. On the wedding day, Echo went out to bring the water for Irene's bridal bath from a sacred spring famous for its pure water. Female relatives chattered and ate sweetmeats in the dining hall as they waited for the bride to appear.

Toward evening she came from the women's courtyard, dressed in a gown of fine white wool, her head covered with a thin veil and crowned with a wreath of winter violets. Petta followed, a tragedy queen in purple and gold. She did not weep, for fear of spoiling her face, but she wrung her hands and moaned that all would go to wrack and ruin without Irene. Kimon offered sacrifices at the family altar and prayed for his daughter in the familiar words: "May the gods grant you all that your heart desires; may they give you a husband and a home and gracious concord, for there is nothing better than this—when a husband and wife keep a household in harmony."

Then in the street there was the sound of voices singing to the music of lyre and flute. The porter threw open the street door and Andreas came in, handsome in a white cloak trimmed with gold. He walked through the house, greeting each of the family with a smile. At last he spoke to Irene in a low voice. Suddenly he picked her up in his arms and ran laughing from the house, while she, laughing too, pretended to struggle. At the door two white oxen were yoked to the marriage cart, their horns gilded and twined with flowers and ribbons. Together, Andreas and his best friend lifted Irene into the cart and leaped in, one on each side of her. Again the music played, the voices sang, and the cart moved off down the street to the bridegroom's house, led by a man with a torch and followed by the bride's family, all bearing torches too. The slaves were left behind.

"I wish I could see the feast," sighed Echo, "and afterward when everyone sings and he leads her away and closes the door. Andreas has a house and garden of his own with plenty of servants and no one to annoy her. How lucky she is."

As Petta had predicted, life in Kimon's house did not go so well after Irene's marriage. Petta took no trouble to see that the corn was kept dry, the wine cool, the floors clean. As the warm weather came on, she again spent time in the courtyard and gave orders, but never took a hand in mixing the flour, kneading the dough, or shaking out cloaks and bedclothes. Instead she trained her monkey to march up and down with a little wicker shield and left household duties to the slaves.

Kimon was displeased but had more important matters on his mind. Rumors continued to come from Asia and the islands. Darius's army were on their way, sailing north along the coast of Asia. They were not expected to come by way of Mount Athos again, because their fleet had been wrecked there in the summer of the Olympic Games. Instead, they would probably cross the Aegean Sea from island to island.

This year Jason went to the farm alone with Thrax to keep him busy in the fields and oversee the work of the slaves. Alexis and Glaukon stayed on in Athens, learning the maneuvers of the infantry and all the ways of using a

157

wicker shield for parrying blows. With the heavily armed men they were trained to attack at a run instead of the usual marching pace. It was a procedure proposed by Miltiades, requiring great precision, since the infantry moved in an unbroken line, eight ranks deep. The shields of the regular infantry were made of oxhide rimmed with bronze, and formed a heavy and solid wall as the army waited for the war cry. At that signal the wall advanced across the field to a rhythmic roar from thousands of throats, "A! La! La! La! La!" The front rank of spears pointed straight forward. Those behind pointed up but were ready for use in battle at a moment's notice if a man in front should fall, killed or wounded. The citizen soldiers sweated in the sun; no race in armor at Olympia was more grueling.

After one of these maneuvers, Alexis was resting at the edge of the field when he saw Telamon standing with a crowd of spectators. There was time for only a moment's talk.

"I thought I might find you here," said Telamon. "I have sent messages to Asini by anyone I met who was going to the Peloponnese. Have you had any word from home?"

"Nothing."

"And now you are going to war. I told you long ago that the Persians would come. They say their ships have already passed Samos, heading west. Why, why did you ever leave home?"

"I have wondered too," Alexis said cheerfully. "But now I think the gods led me here, and I must stay."

"You are too young," Telamon protested.

"Don't look so gloomy," said Alexis. "If I live, I will go home a free man; Kimon has promised. And if I die, do something for me, will you? My grandfather left me the words to the old songs, written down. Tell them at home that I want Melissa's son to have the songs."

Telamon promised.

· 4 ·

The threat of war increased. It was no longer a question of rumors but of facts. Darius's army was commanded by a Mede, Datis, a man famous even in Athens for his ability and courage. His ships had already reached the island of Naxos and subdued it, burning and laying waste all the houses and farms. Datis had taken the men captive and forced them to join their ships to his fleet. Six hundred galleys and transports were now heading toward Eretria on the island of Euboea, separated from Attica only by a narrow channel. As expected, Hippias was with the Persians. He knew every harbor along the coast and would be rewarded for his advice when Athens fell and he became tyrant again.

Now Athens sent a professional runner to Sparta to ask for help. The runner, a man named Pheidippides, covered the distance to Sparta, one hundred and fifty miles, in two days, and returned quickly with good news. The Athenians should send Pheidippides again as soon as the time and place of the Persian landing was certain. Two thousand Spartans would then come at once to join the Greek defense.

On a day of late summer, a man on horseback dismounted at Kimon's door, and knocked. He looked travel-worn and tired, but the porter, impressed by his bearing and look of command, took the horse and said, "Come into

159

the courtyard, sir. The master will soon be home. What is your name and your business?"

"I will tell your master my name and business," said the man.

He did not sit but wandered restlessly about the men's courtyard, watched by the porter, until Kimon arrived from the training ground with Glaukon and Alexis. Then Glaukon cried out, "Father! It can't be! This is a dream!" and he and Neleus were embracing each other, searching for words, while Neleus poured out the fears he had lived with for many months.

At last Kimon spoke a courteous greeting and ordered Geta to bring food and drink. He made Neleus rest in the shade. "Tiryns, Asini, sit with our guest," he said. "Now, tell us, sir, how you found us."

Neleus ate hungrily, never taking his eyes from his son. "Three days ago a sailor came to Tiryns. His name was Milo. He had escaped from a pirate ship and asked for refuge. He told me that I would find my son in Athens. He knew your name, Kimon, and he had followed you to your house when you brought Glaukon here. I have come to buy my son's freedom."

Alexis sat speechless, staring, as Neleus turned to him. "I will buy your freedom too, if Kimon will consent. I have an old debt to pay to your family." He laid a small leather money pouch on the table.

"I will not take your money," Kimon said. "These two earned their own liberty the day they agreed to go to the defense of my country."

"I am king in Tiryns," Neleus said brusquely. "Glaukon is my heir. It will be enough for him to risk his life if the Persians attack Tiryns."

"Forgive me, father, but Alexis and I see it differently," said Glaukon. "If Athens falls, there will be no other defenders from here to the Peloponnese."

Neleus was silent. Then he sighed and said, "You are a man, Glaukon. You must follow your own destiny. And Alexis too, I suppose. Still, you may change your minds. I will leave the money here. I hope it is enough."

"It is enough, whatever it is," said Kimon, "but I will not take it. Since you say you meant to pay an old debt to Asini's family, let it be his." He put his hand on Alexis's shoulder.

"My father would not allow me to accept it," said Alexis. He thought for a moment and turned to Glaukon. "But what your father has done today makes a difference to my family. Let the money be Niki's dowry, if she marries you. The gods may find a way."

So it was settled. Neleus slept that night in Kimon's house and left the next morning to give orders for the defense of Tiryns if the Persians should overrun the Peloponnese.

When Jason returned from the farm he did not want to stay idle with the women and begged his father to let him go with Alexis and Glaukon for military training. But Kimon refused, saying, "If the Persians get past our infantry and attack the city walls, young and old will be needed here. That will be the time for you to play your part."

The mood in Athens was dark. Some rich Athenians, who had much to lose, talked of coming to terms with Darius. Other men went from altar to altar offering prayers and sacrifices, trying to find a priest who would give good omens.

Kimon was scornful. "Since we must fight, what do signs matter? There is only one omen, that a man should fight for his country. Hector said that and was killed be-

161

fore the walls of Troy, but it was a true saying and is
still true."

Then came word that Datis had taken a town at the
southern end of Euboea. His fleet was moving north along
the coast to Eretria. Athens had four thousand armed men
permanently settled in a colony not far to the north. These
men went to the relief of Eretria. They arrived only to
learn that many in that beleaguered city were refusing to
fight. The remnant had sworn to hold out as long as possible, but the soldiers from the Athenian colony took their
advice and withdrew. They sent word to Athens that the
Persians were planning to land at Marathon after the fall
of Eretria. With this news, Pheidippides, the runner, left at
once for Sparta. Marathon was the place where battle
would be joined and the time for Spartan help was now.

Eretria withstood the Persian attack for a week. Then
traitors arranged a surrender, and the defenders with their
wives and children were put on a small island as prisoners.
Next Athens would fall, and Datis would return with all
his captives to Asia. There they would face the wrath and
vengeance of Darius.

Ten thousand Athenians of the heavily armed infantry
immediately started for Marathon, commanded by ten
generals and their commander-in-chief, a citizen named
Callimachus; Kimon went, attended by his free men,
Glaukon and Alexis. Once again they found themselves on
the road to Kimon's farm, but this time they went straight
on to the north, through the fertile valley to the mountain
slopes above Marathon. Before nightfall the Athenians had
made their camp.

We swam here, Alexis thought. But how different that
day had been. Now darkness was spreading over the
mountains on the far side of the bay and on the black

162

expanse of the water. Where the vast Persian fleet lay at anchor, small fires burned as far as the eye could see. The near shore was lit by hundreds of campfires.

The Athenians built their own campfires and ate their supper, friend sitting with friend. Aeschylus brought his young brother to the fire that Alexis and Glaukon had made.

"I am glad you have come," Kimon said, frowning into the dark. "Do you know how many there are down there?"

"Six hundred ships," said Aeschylus, "many of them built and manned by Phoenicians, the best in the world. We have only seventy ships, but we are not fighting at sea. I hear they have landed sixty thousand men, mostly foreign troops forced into Darius's war. We have ten thousand, but we are fighting for our city and for Greece. That makes the difference. And the Spartans will soon be here."

But in the morning, word spread throughout the army that Pheidippides had brought bad news. The Spartans had a custom, a law, as they called it, not to go to war until the moon was full. Then, and not until then, would they come. By daylight the enemy could be seen all too clearly, a swarm covering the entire shore of the crescent-shaped bay, leading horses from the sterns of ships drawn up to the shore, then moving nearer to positions on the plain.

Suddenly Alexis knew that he had seen all of this once before, in his dream at Epidauros. This was the bay; these were the strange ships. Laos, the priest, had said that when this time came, Alexis would be the shield of Achilles. Now the moment had come, and the only shield he had was made of wicker.

In the Athenian camp there were shouts and sounds of confusion. Kimon sent Glaukon to find out what it meant. After some time he returned, panting from his run, and saying, "The generals cannot agree on a plan. Five of them think we should wait for the Spartans; the other five say that we should give battle at once. Callimachus will have to give the deciding vote; Miltiades is talking to him now. Come quickly if you want to hear."

But when they reached the leaders, the conference was over, the decision made. Callimachus had voted with the five generals who wanted to give battle at once. That night, sitting by the campfire, Kimon told what he had heard about Miltiades's powers of persuasion. "He told Callimachus that there were already too many who wanted to abandon Athens without a fight. If we waited for the Spartans, talk of surrender would grow every day, since the longer we sit here looking at the enemy, the more they terrify us. He said that if we save Athens, we can make her the wonder of the world. Now all ten generals have agreed to fight tomorrow."

Alexis, having finished his meal, wrapped himself in his cloak and lay down. Tomorrow would not be another practice at the training ground. Tomorrow would be war itself. Above him in the evening sky, two birds were circling. Now they swooped to the left. Glaukon saw them too.

"A hawk and an eagle," he said under his breath. "They are fighting and they are on the left. I wonder how it will end."

Alexis did not dare to watch. If the birds were an omen, he wanted to put them out of his mind.

Kimon was speaking. "Listen, all of you. These are the orders for tomorrow. Miltiades has been given command for the battle. We will stay here under cover as long as possible so that Datis cannot see how many we are. When the order comes, we are to form the battle line quickly and attack on the run. There is marshland on both sides of the

plain at the shoreline. Keep out of it. There will be an
arrow storm from the Persian archers, but our shield wall
is strong, and our speed will make us a difficult target. We
ourselves will be on the right wing with Callimachus. It is
an honor."

The right wing, thought Alexis. The place of honor,
but the place of danger too. He shivered with a cold no fire
could warm.

"Are you afraid, you young ones?" asked Aeschylus.
"Don't feel ashamed. Every man is afraid before a battle.
But be glad that you are here. Hippias has probably
chosen Marathon for a fight because the plain is what his
cavalry needs, but it is the right place for free Greeks too.
Heroes have fought here, Heracles and Theseus, and many
others. Their spirits surround us and tomorrow they will
cheer us on, as athletes come back to cheer for the new
contenders at Olympia. Sleep well."

Alexis lay listening to the talk of the two men and
wondered if Glaukon and Aeschylus's brother were listening too. Now that they thought the younger ones were
asleep, the older men spoke more freely.

Kimon was saying, "When I was a boy, learning
Homer, my teacher gave me the lines about the falling
leaves. Do you remember? 'A generation of men is like a
generation of leaves: the wind scatters them on the
ground, then spring comes on and there are new leaves on
the trees. So it is with men; the young arise and the old
pass away.' "

"I remember," said Aeschylus. "At Eleusis, where my
family lived, we saw the processions coming every year
with their torches. Then they put out the fires, and as a
child, I was afraid. I knew that the torches would be lit
again and that I would look around and see everyone I

loved, yet I was half dead with fright. That is how I feel even now. When I think of barbed arrows in my flesh, I fear death, and I am already half dead. But the war god is cruel; he takes the young sooner than the old. They go out strong and eager to fight in a war they hardly understand, and they are sent home to their families, a handful of ashes."

"If we die tomorrow, I wonder what it will be like," said Kimon. "Just darkness?"

"Not for the heroes, if the poets are right. You know they tell again and again about how the sun shines there, while we, the living, have night; and about the gardens and the fragrance and fruit, and how we'll be young forever, and join in the singing."

Kimon laughed softly. "Then let's be heroes." He turned on his side and slept.

But I am no hero, thought Alexis. Will I lie in the dark earth and end as a ghost, gibbering on the other side of the river Styx?

He opened his eyes and saw the rim of light over the mountains of Euboea. Somehow the night had passed and already Glaukon was fastening the buckles of Kimon's breastplate. They made a hasty meal of bread and wine, standing about the dead campfire. Then they heard shouts echoing from the hillside and coming closer.

"Alexis, find out what is happening," said Kimon. "Quickly. We should not be imagining every possible disaster."

Alexis's heart felt hollow, but he strapped on his sword. Picking up his shield, he headed along the line of Athenian campfires where other groups of men had heard the shouting too and were anxiously looking toward the north. Now that he was in motion, he felt less afraid, but he kept under cover as he went on. He had not gone far before he reached some soldiers who were grinning and raising clenched fists in the air. They told him what he needed to know.

"The Plataeans! The Plataeans have come! A thousand of them!"

"I never heard of Plataea. Where is it?" he asked.

A man clapped him on the back. "Plataea? You don't know much, do you? It's northwest of here, not far. We went to help them in some war of theirs a few years back, and now every fighting man they have has come to help us. We didn't even ask them to come. The lion and the mouse, that's what it is!"

Alexis carried the amazing news back along the line, followed by cheers all the way. Kimon and Aeschylus were jubilant. "You can tell what the Plataeans have done for us," said Aeschylus. "Listen to the shouting. Now the priests will be giving good omens, wait and see."

Early in the afternoon, word was passed along the line that the combined infantry should form their shield wall on the plain. They moved quickly into position, the Plataeans on the left, and Callimachus with the strongest detachment of Athenians on the right. In the center, the Athenian line was thin, but their general, Themistocles, was one of the best, and had special orders to turn their weakness into an asset. If the center had to retreat, they were to withdraw into the hills, using the trees and rocks as cover, and there fight to the death.

From north to south across the plain, the Greek shield wall now stood, topped with the gleam of helmets. Behind this wall stood another, the light-armed free men of Athens, craftsmen, artisans, men who owned nothing but little booths in the marketplace, slaves who had won their freedom by coming to fight at Marathon. With these stood Alexis and Glaukon, keeping their eyes on Kimon's helmet in the front rank. All were motionless, waiting for the shout that would signal the attack.

From the level plain Alexis could no longer see the Persians. When will they see us? he wondered. I should say a prayer. But to which god, and what should I pray? Then he found words. "When you come to the place of battle, where the best men fight, do not bring shame on your father's house or on us who in time past have been famous for strength and courage in all the world." He prayed to whatever gods might be listening, and asked for strength and courage.

Somewhere in front of him a trumpet blared and with it Alexis heard the war cry of Miltiades. The sound was picked up by every man until earth and sky seemed driven together by the roar and Alexis heard the sound coming from his own throat. "A! La! La! La! La!" The helmet crests were moving and the shield wall clashed as the long line swept forward. Thousands of spears caught the light.

Then came an answering shout. The mounted Persian archers were coming to meet them, and the storm of arrows was aimed at the center. They pelted like hail against the leather shields. Still advancing behind the right wing, Alexis saw the Athenian center begin to give away. They were breaking and retreating toward the hills, followed by the mounted archers of the enemy. But the right wing continued its advance and the Plataeans were closing the gap. Now battle was joined all along the front and the Greek shield wall stopped, halted by the impact of the Persian onslaught. A few men in the front rank fell, but Kimon's helmet was still visible. Then the men at the front were moving forward again. Alexis, at the rear, could see

little of the fighting. He only knew that the Greek spears were taking their toll, for as they advanced, the plain was strewn with dead and wounded Persians and their horses.

Dusk was falling, and on the decks of the Persian ships torches burned. Then, over the din of battle, shouts came from the mountainside. "Into the sea! Drive them into the sea!" Alexis saw Athenian soldiers coming from the hills behind him. No Persians, only Athenians. Among the trees and rocks of their own hills the soldiers of the center had annihilated the invaders and were returning to finish the fight. Their cry was taken up—"Drive them into the sea!" —and the line surged forward again. The earth seemed to tremble as if the deathless feet of some god were striding toward the sea.

Suddenly the front line parted and the light-armed infantry heard the word for which they had been waiting: "Advance at the run!" They poured into the open plain and Alexis saw what had been hidden by the shield wall. The Persians were in chaos. Seized by panic they were running, stumbling, falling, in headlong flight to the ships, many drowning in the marsh.

Other runners were ahead of Alexis, racing toward the ships, some heavily armed infantrymen throwing down their shields to be free of the great weight. They ran with javelins and swords in hand. Alexis sped forward with Glaukon beside him. "But I will reach the ships first," Alexis said to himself. The Persian archers were clambering aboard their ships and sailors were hacking at the anchor ropes.

Alexis gathered all his energy for a sprint, and, as at Olympia, his muscles obeyed his will. He left Glaukon behind and was overtaking other runners, nearing the ships. Then he felt the strength coming as it had come at

169

Olympia. It seemed to come from the earth around him and from the sky and sea, and he was part of all these. "I am Heracles, I am Theseus, I am Diomedes of the loud war cry, I belong to Zeus!" Had the voice come from him with his own breathing, or had other voices spoken? He did not know, but now he was the first of all the pursuing Greeks and the beach lay just ahead. He ran toward the nearest of the ships—a Phoenician vessel, to judge by its looks. From the deck a javelin arched and fell at his feet. He picked it up and ran on to the edge of the water. There Glaukon passed him, sword in hand, without his shield. Above them Alexis saw a sailor with a burning torch poised for the throw. He hurled the javelin and the man toppled into the sea, throwing the torch into Glaukon's face even as he fell. Glaukon caught it and hurled it back; not for nothing had he ridden the torch race in days of peace. The torch fell among ropes on the deck of the ship.

A Persian archer floundered through the water and scrambled to the deck. Alexis saw him fit an arrow to his bow and take aim at Glaukon. He threw himself against Glaukon, knocking him to his knees in the water. Then he felt the arrow tearing into his own chest. He cried out, and fell.

In his ears were the screams and groans of other voices, cursing and pleading in unknown languages. He gasped with pain, choking in the salt water for a moment that seemed an eternity. Then he dragged himself up the shelving beach and lay still. The ship was burning; the flames glared against the sky. After that came darkness and unbearable thirst, and pain.

·VII·

To Asini

·1·

T HE BAY was calm in the early morning light. The tide was out, leaving the sand smooth all along the shore. Only the feet of the two runners had left a mark, the boy's stride almost as long as the man's. Now the two sat on a stone resting and looking across the blue water toward the little island where the columns of the new temple to Poseidon stood against the sky. The man had talked and now was silent.

"What happened then?" urged the boy. "Go on, Alexis."

The man laughed. "But I have told you many times. You know it all by heart. And if you are late for school, you will get a beating."

"No, tell it again. I have a holiday today for the thirteenth anniversary of Marathon."

"Good. Well, then. Glaukon carried me off the battlefield and took me to the doctors. They had made a shelter for the wounded near an old shrine to Heracles on the hill, and Andreas was there. He gave me wine and the juice of poppies to ease the pain. Then he cut out the arrow and washed my wound. He put herbs on it and bound it up. After a while it stopped bleeding."

"Then they took you to Athens."

173

"True, on a litter, and that was terrible. But they carried me to Kimon's house and I was well cared for there."

The boy hesitated, then asked a question he had never quite dared to ask. "Did Irene ever come?"

"She came once with Andreas, while I was sleeping. She made the medicines he gave me. Others weren't so lucky."

The boy frowned, thinking it out. "If you had all stayed behind the shield wall, you might not have been wounded."

"But then the Persians would have got away to their ships. As it was, our infantry left more than six thousand of them dead on the field. They say Datis thought we were madmen when he saw how few we were, but when he saw what those few did, he thought differently. We lost only a hundred and ninety-two of the heavily armed infantry, mostly in the attack on the ships. That's where Aeschylus was wounded and his brother killed."

"The Spartans should have come."

"I've told you why they didn't get there in time. When they came and saw the six thousand, men from countries you and I never heard of, men with long hair, some with their hair in braids, strangely dressed, many half naked, they said we had done well. Then they went home."

"But they should have come in time," the boy insisted.

"They did better afterward. Three hundred of them died defending the pass at Thermopylae, the year of Salamis. I ran against a Spartan at Olympia, and I have wondered whether he was at Thermopylae. His name was Lampis."

"Tell about the Athenians after Marathon."

"They marched back to Athens that night. When the

174

Persian fleet came to Phaleron the next day, there were the same men they had just fought, drawn up on the heights, ready to fight again."

"That ended it for Datis," said the boy, sighing with satisfaction.

"And for Darius too. He died, and his son Xerxes took his place, but for ten years we had time to get ready for whatever Xerxes might do. Well, silver mines were discovered in Attica and there was talk of dividing the money among all the citizens of Athens. But Themistocles wouldn't have it that way. Remember, he had commanded the center at Marathon and knew how close we had come to defeat. He is a man who makes people listen. So Athens built its navy and opened up new harbors. Then came Salamis. I don't need to tell you about Salamis."

"Of course not. I remember when the news came here about the great naval victory and about Xerxes himself there on the island, seeing his ships destroyed. I remember how we all laughed and danced."

"There was no laughing and dancing in Athens. The Persians burned it. But already it is being rebuilt, finer than ever, they say, with new temples, a new theater, new houses. Some day you and I must see it together. I'll show you Kimon's house, if it still stands. We may see him."

"Could we see Irene?"

"I wouldn't try. But since you ask, I did see her once, about three years ago, not long after Salamis. The women and children were all sent out of Athens to the Peloponnese before the Persians burned the city and many of them went to Troezen. It's not far south of Epidauros, you know. And after the victory there was a great celebration of thanksgiving at Epidauros. I went, and I saw Irene with her husband. They must have stopped there on their way back to Athens. They were standing looking at the great statue and they didn't see me."

"Why didn't you speak to them?"

"They didn't need me. Ten years had passed. They would hardly have known me with my beard. . . . No, that's not it. I don't know why I didn't speak."

"I hope I'll never have to go through all that has happened to you," the boy said. "To be a slave and be branded, to fight with all the odds against you and to have so much pain. I couldn't do so well as you did."

"Yes, you could. You will, if you have to. Don't be afraid of what may come to you, Alexis. 'We learn by suffering.' Aeschylus said that in one of his poems, and it's worth knowing by heart. 'We learn by suffering. Instead of sleep, painful memories fall like rain on the heart, but wisdom comes even to those who do not want it, a gift that cannot be refused, because it is from the gods, who steer our course.' Yet what happened to me was my own doing, and I would not change it, even if I could."

The boy spoke as if he were telling a shameful secret. "If I had to fight, I'm afraid I might run away."

"As for fighting, I hope we've won a peace that will last for my lifetime and yours. But if you have to protect your homeland, you would go forward with a stout heart. The Fates do the spinning and the weaving, Alexis. Until they cut the thread, don't fear life, don't fear death. Aeschylus is famous now, you know, but when he dies, he wants nothing on his tombstone about his plays, only that he fought at Marathon. Pheidippides fought through the battle and then ran with the last of his strength to Athens with the glorious news. That final run killed him, but it was a happy death."

"Can we see Marathon some day?" asked the boy.

"Of course. We'll see the mound where they buried the Plataeans, and the one they raised for the freed slaves. Those are on the battlefield, and I'll show you where Glaukon and I stood. Nearer the sea is the mound where the Athenian infantry were buried, with their names written on columns all around."

The older Alexis stood up. "Shall we go to the promontory? I want to give thanks that I came home."

As they walked along the beach and climbed the stone stairway, he went on, "Our mother never loses hope that father will come home, you know. She says to me that Odysseus was gone for twenty years after Troy, and came home at last. But if Aristes never comes back, she has Dion and you and me, and someday we will marry, and the house will be full. And I think Chrysis and Gorgo are immortal. Best of all, Niki is happy with Glaukon at Tiryns. It's strange how the gods found a way to heal the old feud. It's like the end of a long sickness. Melissa can hardly ask for more. Except for Aristes. She will always want Aristes. But some prayers are not answered."

They walked out to the graves of the old man and the child and said a prayer for them and for Aristes. They gave thanks for life.

"You brought Abas's sword home," said the boy.

"And you have the songs that he wrote down for me. What is your lesson for tomorrow? Will you say it for me?"

They turned back toward the house. "I'll try," the young Alexis said. "We have just come to the long passage about the shield that the lame god made for Achilles: 'He made a shield great and strong, adorned all over, five folds thick and with a rim heavy and shining. And on it he pictured the earth, and the heavens, and the sea, and the

177

unwearying sun, and the full moon and all the stars.' " He went on without faltering as he described the marvel of the shield. " 'In another part, workers were reaping with sharp sickles while behind them boys gathered up the grain and carried it to the binders, and among them the king was standing at the swathe, rejoicing in his heart.' "

"That is it," said the man. "You have it perfectly, Alexis. You make me see the shield of Achilles, advancing before us at Marathon. But the wicker shields were there, too. They followed, and they did their part. Yes, Alexis, my namesake, the wicker shields did their part."